McCracken
and the
Lost Cavern

Our tank topped the rise. For a moment, the front third of the tank rose over it, its belly exposed. I couldn't see what was happening outside, but I touched the rosary in my breast pocket and prayed silently.

We didn't hear the German anti-tank rifle fire; our engine was far too loud for that. But the sound of it puncturing the skin of the tank floor rang in our ears. Shrapnel exploded through the front half of the cabin. Hamilton and I were both thrown to the side; as he fell, Hamilton pulled the firing pin and the six-pounder went off with a boom, ejecting the empty shell onto the floor.

Silence fell upon us. The anti-tank gun's bullet had ripped a hole through the underside of the tank and exploded inside, riddling the engine with shrapnel. Smoke began to fill the compartment.

Coughing, we picked ourselves up from the floor. The Chief Gunner, a gruff sergeant called Macklethwaite, peered through his vision slit.

"Half a dozen Hun closing in," he said. "Looks like the end of the War for us."

Also by Mark Adderley

The Hawk and the Wolf
The Hawk and the Cup
The Hawk and the Huntress

For Young Readers:
McCracken and the Lost Island
McCracken and the Lost Valley
McCracken and the Lost City
McCracken and the Lost Lagoon
McCracken and the Lost Lady

McCracken and the Lost Cavern

By Mark Adderley

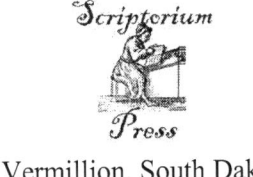

Vermillion, South Dakota
2018

© 2018 by Mark Adderley
All rights reserved

Published by Scriptorium Press,
Vermillion, South Dakota

To Sadie

Contents

Chapter 1.	A Meeting in No-Man's Land	1
Chapter 2.	Back at the Front	11
Chapter 3.	Schools and Canned Food	26
Chapter 4.	In the Study	41
Chapter 5.	The Flying Scotsman	54
Chapter 6.	Welcome to Scotland	65
Chapter 7.	The Gathering	78
Chapter 8.	The Card Sharp	91
Chapter 9.	Highland Games	102
Chapter 10.	The Castle	114
Chapter 11.	Into the Maze	129
Chapter 12.	Spies and Stalagmites	143
Chapter 13.	The Steel Prison	157
Chapter 14.	In the Drink	171
Chapter 15.	Ari's Story	185
Chapter 16.	An Eleventh-Hour Solution	196
From Fritz's Kitchen		204

CHAPTER 1
A MEETING IN NO-MAN'S LAND

Our Mark V-Star tank lumbered across no-man's land, a wilderness of mud and shell-holes between the forward trenches of the German Army (before us) and the British (behind us). Inside, the eight crewmembers and myself, a civilian observer, were locked into a compartment of grey-painted steel, in the middle of which the 150-horsepower Ricardo engine thundered away, churning out fumes that had begun to make us faint before we were halfway between the trenches. I looked up to where the tiny fan, directly above the engine, spun valiantly, extracting just too little of the noxious air for comfort.

"Excuse me, Wullie," I said to the gunner beside me, as I tried to press past him towards where the driver and commander sat.

Willie Hamilton, a fellow Scot from the east coast, peered through his gun-sight, drinking the external air deeply, but he jumped so he hit his head when I tapped him on the shoulder. He said something in his northern dialect that thankfully I couldn't hear over the pulsing sound of the engine, then leaned closer. "Sorry, McCracken, I didnae hear you over the bloody Sassenach engine!"

I frowned. Hamilton looked greenish around the eyes and in the cheeks. The fumes were beginning to claim him. I nodded and moved on towards the forward positions in the cabin. "Captain!" I called.

Captain Lampton-Pitt, a fiery fellow with a neat ginger moustache and startling blue eyes, turned to me, his eyebrow rising under the peak of his officer's cap.

"Captain," I said, "may I respectfully suggest we turn about and return to our lines?" I jerked a thumb over my shoulder. "The men are severely affected by the engine fumes."

"Then why am I not, McCracken?" demanded Lampton-Pitt.

I gestured past him. "You receive sufficient circulation through the forward vision slit, sir," I pointed out. "The men don't have that benefit."

Lampton-Pitt sighed and stared through the vision slit. A line of barbed wire, looped in great circles about rugged posts, stretched out through the mud and craters on either side. "We're so close, McCracken," he said. "Our orders are to reach enemy positions, fire at least four volleys, and then return."

"I understand that, sir," I replied, "but I believe I've seen enough to assess the performance of the Mark V-Star. There's insufficient ventilation so the crew gets quickly ill, and the engine is so loud the crewmembers can't communicate with one another. Also, the engine heat is too extreme. With respect, we've fulfilled our mission."

Lampton-Pitt waved a gloved finger through the vision slit. "Look. The Hun trenches—bally things were ours just a couple of days ago—are just on the other side of that ridge. Let's try just a bit longer, eh?"

"As you say, Captain." I returned to Willie Hamilton's side. He was leaning on his Hotchkiss six-pounder, fanning himself with one hand. He looked up and smiled weakly at me.

"Do you think, McCracken, they will issue tankers with gas-masks in days tae come?" he said with a smile.

At that moment, a loud *clang!* echoed through the tank's cabin, as if someone had struck the outside of the vehicle with a mallet.

"Great Scott!" I cried. "What on earth was that?"

I hurried forward to Lampton-Pitt. He motioned again through the vision slit. "There he is, the blighter!" he announced as a bright flash showed just above the rise we were about to climb. Another impact rang out as, beside us, the front gunner squeezed his trigger and let out a three-second burst.

"A Tankgewehr," I said. Lampton-Pitt nodded vigorously. We both knew from our briefing before the mission that the Germans had developed an anti-tank rifle, large and difficult to fire but theoretically able to punch through the armour of British tanks. I wished I could get out and look at the damage, but two hits appeared to have made no holes in us.

"Blighter's probably scarpered," commented Lampton-Pitt, leaning close and yelling in my ear. "Williams scared him off, I shouldn't wonder."

"There was a double-clang on the last hit."

"Yes." Lampton-Pitt smiled with satisfaction. "Glanced off the front armour plating and ricocheted off the front panel. They'll have to try harder than that."

"Twelve-millimetre armour," I reflected quietly, and did a quick mental calculation: the armour plating on the front of the Mark V sloped, so its thickness was increased by the angle and the square root of two. That meant that if a bullet from the Tankgewehr struck the tank square on it would actually have to penetrate seventeen millimetres of armour plating. Nothing could get through that. But when we climbed the rise, the underside of the tank would for a few moments be exposed. I pointed this out.

"I shouldn't worry about it, McCracken," answered Lampton-Pitt. "We're moving pretty fast, you know—we're making almost five miles per hour."

I staggered a little as I returned to Hamilton's side. The front machine-gun rattled away, again and again. Hamilton cranked his gun around so it was facing forward. The floor of the tank began to slope as we climbed the rise.

"I see a pair of Huns!" Hamilton shouted. "Captain Lampton-Pitt! I see a pair of Huns!"

"Corporal Hamilton!" yelled Lampton-Pitt, spinning around. "Did you say something?"

"Yes sir!" shouted Hamilton, over the pulsing of the engine. "Two Huns, starboard fifteen degrees."

"Open fire!" shouted Lampton-Pitt.

Hamilton's elbow jabbed in and out as he cranked the barrel of his six-inch gun down on the Germans. His eye was fixed on the scope.

We topped the rise. For a moment, the front third of the tank rose over it, its belly exposed. I couldn't see what was happening outside, but I touched the rosary in my breast pocket and prayed silently.

We didn't hear the German anti-tank rifle fire; our engine was far too loud for that. But the sound of it puncturing the skin of the tank floor rang in our ears. Shrapnel exploded through the front half of the cabin. Hamilton and I were both thrown to the side; as he fell, Hamilton pulled the firing pin and the six-pounder went off with a boom, ejecting the empty shell onto the floor.

Silence fell upon us. The Tankgewehr's bullet had ripped a hole through the underside of the tank and exploded inside, killing Lampton-Pitt, the driver and the forward machine-gunner and then riddling the engine. Smoke began to fill the compartment.

Coughing, we picked ourselves up from the floor—six survivors. Miraculously, neither Hamilton nor I were even wounded, and I said a quick prayer of thanks. The Chief Gunner, a gruff sergeant called Macklethwaite, peered past the still form of the forward gunner and through his vision slit.

"Half a dozen Hun closing in. Looks like the end of the War for us." He turned to me. "What will you do, Mr. McCracken?"

"I don't know—I'll think of something." An idea occurred to me. "With your permission, Sergeant." He nodded. "Do you have a couple of Mill's Bombs?" I asked, holding out my hand. Somebody found two hand grenades and placed them in my palm. We could hear German voices from outside. A brutal knocking rang on the exit hatch and a guttural voice demanded, "*Kommt raus! Übergebt euch!*"

"Get your rifles," I said. "Get ready to exit. We're going to have to cross no-man's land on foot."

While they got ready, I pulled the body of the unfortunate gunner from his seat and leaned him against the engine bulkhead. Then, climbing into the spot he had occupied, I yanked the pin out of one hand grenade and tossed it through the vision slit to the left. I heard a soft *ding!* as it struck the edge of the tank and bounced.

"*Granate!*" came a shriek from outside. We could hear a flurry of motion.

"Now—the hatch!" I cried. "Don't open it until—"

Macklethwaite's hand was on the handle when the roar of the grenade shook the tank. The sergeant pushed on the door and the four other survivors of the tank crew piled out, rifles at the ready. I stood behind them, a Scott-Webley revolver in one hand, the second hand grenade, already primed, in the other.

Two Germans lay dead; another four staggered about in the mud. It seemed unsporting to kill them. "Let's go," I said.

"Sir—the tank." Macklethwaite looked anxious. "We can't leave it for the Hun."

"Right," I said. I held up the grenade. "I can blow her up with this, but we'll need to remove the bodies."

Macklethwaite gave me a nod and turned to the others. "You two cover the Germans. Hamilton, Smith, you remove the bodies from inside."

It took a few moments, and all the time I had to hold the grenade's handle firmly down so it wouldn't explode. But at last the bodies of our three comrades lay beside the tank. I tossed the grenade inside and slammed the hatch shut. A few second later, an explosion sounded inside and smoke trailed out through the vision slits and gun ports.

"Sergeant, what will we do with the prisoners?" I asked. "We can't take them back to our lines."

"That we can't, sir, but we can't leave them here to shoot us in the backs neither."

"I've an idea. With your permission, Sergeant?"

Again, Macklethwaite nodded, and I picked up one of the rifles belonging to a German soldier. It was a Gewehr 98, a perfectly serviceable gun and standard issue in the German Army. With a couple of quick motions, I removed the bolt and threw it as far away from me as I could. I handed it back to its owner and held out my hand, palm-up. "*Bajonett, bitte*," I said. A forlorn expression on his face—he couldn't have been more than sixteen years old—he slid his bayonet out of its sheath and handed it to me. I hurled it after the bolt. Grinning, the tankers closed in and disarmed the rest of the Germans similarly.

"I think I'll keep this, sir, if you don't think it would be a problem." Sergeant Macklethwaite hefted the Tankgewehr. It was a remarkable gun—nearly six feet long, with a pistol grip and bipod.

I nodded. "Our chaps will find it most interesting," I agreed.

The Germans were now disarmed. Hamilton took one German's entrenching tool away from him, then pointed to the bodies of our dead comrades and of the Germans. "You bury them respectfully," he said loudly. The Germans looked at us with wrinkled brows beneath their steel helmets. I frowned—they weren't spiked, like the helmets I had seen earlier in the War, and some of them were camouflaged in green, rust and tan.

One of the tank crew took the entrenching tool from Hamilton and handed it back to the German. "*Begraben*," he said, pointing. "*Ja?*"

The German nodded. "*Ja.*"

We paused a moment, saluting our fallen comrades. But then a gunshot sounded from the direction of the German trenches, galvanizing Macklethwaite into action. "They're coming after us, sir," he said urgently. "Come on!"

A few seconds later we were dashing away, back across the most dangerous quarter-mile in the world.

Chapter 2
Back at the Front

Moments before, we had been six soldiers who had just scored a victory over the enemy. Now we became human animals, hugging the folds of the grey earth, occasionally swallowed by wreaths of smoke, darting from one hollow in the ground to another, sometimes bent at the waist, sometimes scrambling on all fours. We began to look like the mud through which we crawled.

From time to time machine-guns would chatter harshly from the German lines, and then we would roll into a ditch, hide behind a blasted tree, or just curl up under our helmets and pray they would miss us. We had to slow down soon, because we had reached the barbed wire, curling between slanted uprights to the left and right as far as the eye could see. We had no wire clippers, so we squeezed ourselves into the mud and wriggled under the terrible stuff. I could feel the evil little spikes snagging at my clothing, and the terror rose in me: I knew that if I pulled hard to loosen it, that would just make it worse. I worked methodically and slowly to free myself from the steel grip of the wire, while bullets whistled by and shells shrieked overhead. Sweat sprang on my forehead even though it was the end of March, and bitterly cold. "Thank you, God," I said, as one barb released me; "thank you, God," as another one sprang away.

Then I was free, running at a crouch again. At the sound of gunfire from behind, I threw myself into a foxhole, reddish water gushing up all about me. I was with Hamilton, whose teeth gleamed white in the middle of his blackened face. His eyes dropped to my leg.

"I ken you've been wounded, Mr. McCracken," he said with a nod.

I looked down, and saw that my trousers had been snagged by a bullet, three inches above my left knee. The trousers were soaked with blood, and now I could feel the dull pain of the wound. Hamilton took my scarf and made it into a bandage, which managed to slow down the bleeding.

"Can you move, sir?"

I flexed my muscles. "It's not a deep wound," I said. Hamilton nodded. Then, with a grin, he vaulted up the side of the foxhole and ran on. I stood, dripping, and followed him. The wounded leg slowed me, but not too much. I was too scared to be still.

Moments later, we rolled over some sandbags and sprawled on the filthy floor of a British trench, not much more really than a shallow depression in the ground. We were surrounded by Tommies, whose firm hands hauled us to our feet. We were safe.

"Tankers?" one asked. We nodded. "Lost your commander?" We nodded again.

"What are you doing here?" demanded an almost squeaky voice, and we found that a captain with bright shoulder-pips had elbowed his way through the crowd to us.

"Macklethwaite, Sergeant, D Company Tank Corps," barked our sergeant, snapping out a salute.

The captain returned his salute. "What are your orders?"

"Assess the viability of the Mark V-Star, fire volleys at enemy positions, return to British lines, sir. Tank destroyed, captain killed in action, sir."

The captain winced. "I see. Then you'll be wanting to get back to your positions. Where are you stationed?"

But before Macklethwaite could answer, something screeched overhead. With a massive noise like thunder, the earth quivered; black smoke boiled upwards. I threw myself to the ground, like everyone else around me. The ground seemed to jump up and hit me in the face. Grass and sod pattered down to earth all around us. For a moment, the world was silent, then sound returned, as if I were surfacing from deep water.

"Enemy bombardment, sir!" shouted one of the Tommies.

"Fix bayonets!" called out the captain. "Prepare for attack!" Turning to us, he added, "Might be a bit dangerous to go back to your billets right now. Better stay with us. Foster will issue you rifles."

A private shoved rifles and bayonets into our hands as the shells exploded all around us, spattering our heads with clods of earth. The bombardment was endless now, and my ears rang with the constant detonations.

After one particularly close call, just a few yards in front of us, one of the Tommies whistled. "One of ours," he said. "At least we know they're firing back."

"That was close," I observed. "Can't they aim?"

"Oh yes, sir," he replied. "But the guns is so worn and smooth with use that they often comes closer to us than to Fritz, sir."

The captain was staring, oddly enough, back. I followed his line of sight. The German shells were landing way behind our own lines now. "They're targeting our artillery," he mused. He consulted his watch. "Where are those French reinforcements they promised?" he demanded.

"Look." Private Foster pointed. "There's one of the blighters now, getting ready to attack. Enemy in sight, sir!"

"What happened to the spikes on their helmets?" I asked.

The Tommy did a double-take. "I see you haven't been on the Front in a while, sir," he said, holding his rifle close. "They haven't been wearing them spikes for—oh, it must be getting on three years now."

"Why did they stop wearing them?"

Another of the Tommies called up from the bottom of the trench: "Some friend of the Kaiser's put his helmet on a chair, and Kaiser Bill sat on it!" There was laughter for a few moments, then the spotter said: "I think, sir, those spiked helmets made good targets for our boys. All you had to do was aim three inches below the spike and *boom!* Like shooting apples out of a tree, sir."

He cocked his head. Dirt fell round about for a few seconds, but no more explosions followed. "That was a short one," he commented.

"Following their recent pattern. There will be Stormtroopers soon, I warrant," put in the captain.

There was a flurry of activity, and someone with a Lewis gun ran forward and set it up at the edge of the trench. "The other machine-gun post got a direct hit, sir," he explained. "They was targeting us." Immediately, the corporal wielding the gun lined up his eye along the sights and let loose a staccato coughing as the muzzle flashed fire. A staggered volley of rifle fire joined it. I peered over the line of sandbags at the top of the trench, and saw the skyline filled with figures clad in field grey, their heads misshapen by the great square helmets. One of them flung his arms wide and fell over backwards. Another one went down.

Then they were on us.

The next few moments were savage and bitter. We fought with bullets and bayonets, but even more the edge of a shovel or the butt of a rifle, and blood mingled with mud. I saw a face before me, smeared with dirt, topped by the square green helmet. A rifle thrust at me, but I knocked it aside. The soldier leaped at me and we grappled. But a moment later, he arched over backwards, and above us stood Willie Hamilton. A bayonet was in his hand, the blade dark. The German soldier was still, and only then did I see how young he had been.

"There they go, lads!" came a voice. And indeed, the Germans were running. The corporal re-mounted the Lewis and started rattling off after them. Far more fell when they ran than when they were advancing.

"Well done, brave lads!" The captain was re-holstering his revolver. "They'll be back, I shouldn't wonder—it's their pattern the last few days. But not immediately." He turned to us. "You chaps had better get back to your positions while there's a breather."

So we took leave of the Tommies in the trench and started slogging off through the mud towards the rear of the line. "Not much of a trench, that," I pointed out.

"The Hun have never pushed us back so far." Sergeant Macklethwaite waved his arm about. "This is where we fought nearly two years ago, the Somme. Never thought we'd be fighting here again. But the Hun have advanced very quickly the last few days, so they have, sir." After a few moments of silence, he said, "I don't know if you're a praying man, sir, but today is Palm Sunday—the third I've spent on the Front. Makes you think, doesn't it? Did Our Lord know He was going to die a few days' hence, when He rode that donkey? And how do we know we'll see Easter?"

"Palm Sunday today?" I didn't comment on his theology. I had lost track of the days, and didn't like the fact that I had been working, fighting even, on the Lord's Day.

We trudged on. A platoon of blue-uniformed French soldiers passed us, their unshaven faces staring wide-eyed beneath the brims of their strange helmets. There weren't many of them, and I reflected that the reinforcements the captain back in the trench expected would disappoint him somewhat. They gave us sloppy salutes.

"*Bonjour*," said Hamilton as we passed.

"'Allo, Tommies," replied one of the French soldiers.

On we went, a line of trees, shattered and leafless, growing steadily ahead of us. Between the trees, I could see the outlines of large howitzers. Smoke curled about the trees, and flashes of fire lit it up as the guns boomed and spat their deadly shot over the miles between them and the German guns. As we approached, an enemy shell screamed overhead and detonated right next to one of the guns. The fire and the fountain of dirt and debris that rose from it blinded us for a moment, and I threw myself to the ground. I felt stones and bits of earth drumming all about like rain against a windowpane. I looked up.

None of the others had taken cover, and it was with a feeling of sheepishness that I got to my feet.

"That was a close one," commented Hamilton.

Then we were running again—running as fast as we could towards the friendly artillery, praying that no German shell would fall short and kill us all. My wounded leg throbbed with pain, and my comrades passed me one by one.

Because of the cacophony of the bombardment, I didn't hear the German plane until the twin Spandau machine guns opened up. Fountains of dirt erupted on either side of me as the bullets smacked into the earth. One of our crew ahead of me went down. The plane roared overhead, the triple wings identifying it as a Fokker Dr. I, but it wasn't blazing red, it wasn't the famous Red Baron. The Dr. I swept up and banked left. It would swing around and home in for another strafing run.

For the most part, pilots thought it unchivalrous to fire on human ground targets. But as the War had dragged on, everyone got more and more brutal and desperate. I ran on, my heart pounding so powerfully that it felt as if it were knocking against the inside of my ribs. I thought my wounded leg would give way at any moment.

Another sound came from behind us: the engine of another plane, but a different, slightly smoother timbre from the Dr. I. Looking back, I saw the double wings and snub nose of a wholly different model: it was a Nieuport 17, a French plane, but as it flashed roaring over our heads, I saw it bore British markings. It banked left after the Dr. I and opened up with a quick burst. The remainder of our crew paused and cheered, throwing our fists up in the air. Sergeant Macklethwaite nudged my elbow and pointed up. The sky was full of planes, wheeling, circling, diving, soaring up into the clouds. Some of them trailed long clouds of pungent smoke. One turned over slowly, one of its wings detaching as we watched.

"Our boys'll drive 'em off, all right," commented Macklethwaite. "Come on, lads!"

Hamilton and another of the crew picked up the fallen tanker, and a few minutes later, me limping dreadfully, we reached the lines of guns. The roar as they fired was continuous and deafening.

"Who the devil are you?" A gunnery major strode towards us, waving his swagger stick threateningly.

"Macklethwaite, Sergeant, D Company Tank Corps," said the Sergeant once more. "Tank disabled, sir. Reporting back to headquarters."

The swagger stick flashed out and pointed behind the firing line. "There are some ambulances and lorries there. One of them will take you where you need to go. There's a burial detail there too—you can leave your casualty with them. Any of you wounded?"

"Slight leg wound, sir." Macklethwaite pointed to me.

"It just needs cleaning and a bandage—nothing deep," I said.

"Captain and three others killed in action," Macklethwaite went on. "The rest of us, just scratches, sir."

"Very good. Well, carry on, Sergeant."

Macklethwaite gave him a smart salute, and we all made our way to where he had pointed. A small collection of ambulances and lorries stood around, their motors idling. One of the ambulances pulled away as we arrived. Wounded and dead soldiers were lined up, and Hamilton and the other tanker laid down their comrade at the end of the line. We stood around the still form for a few moments, our helmets off. I made the Sign of the Cross.

"Let's see that leg, dear," said a nurse, as we made our way towards the lorries. She rolled up the leg of my trousers, cleaned the wound and bound it firmly with a bandage. I thanked her and joined Macklethwaite, Hamilton and the others in a lorry that was going to Amiens. Shortly afterwards, the lorry started bouncing over the rutted surface of the dirt road.

Macklethwaite looked at me with concern. "Are you all right, Mr. McCracken, sir?"

I blinked, finding myself the centre of attention. "I think so, Sergeant, thank you. I've been in plenty of fights before, but never a battle. How do you manage?"

Sergeant Macklethwaite puffed out his cheeks. "I can't really say as I knows, sir. A man can get used to anything, I reckon. What I wonders is, how am I going to get used to civilian life after all this mucking around in France?"

Amiens had been bombed almost continually during the War, and had changed hands a couple of times. But still the medieval cathedral stood proud above the ruins, damaged and blackened in places, but still a testament to the eternal life of that over which the gates of hell would never prevail. All around were the empty shells of buildings, many still roofed, but none without some kind of damage or other. The lorry dropped us off in a cobbled street where an expanse of grass led to a building that looked as if it had been built just before the French Revolution. Still the cathedral towered over us. The lawn was covered with British soldiers, reclining or sitting in groups. They were hungrily shoveling food out of cans into their mouths and laughing, talking, gesturing.

"What's going on?" wondered Hamilton.

Macklethwaite grinned. "Don't you know, Wullie? Look." He pointed. "It's Sir Tim!"

Moving about the reclining soldiers was a man about whom flapped a long army greatcoat, as if he were an officer, and he carried a swagger stick. But he wore neither cap nor rank insignia. The brown boots were military issue, and only slightly soiled with mud. His hair was grey like steel, and slicked close to his skull, his features heavy and fleshy. His lips flashed smiles left and right at the soldiers.

"Sir Tim?"

"That's right, Mr. McCracken." Macklethwaite warmed to his topic. "Haven't you heard of Sir Timothy LaGrange, sir? He's a, what you may call him, a philatelist."

"He collects stamps?"

"No, sir, not stamps. He does good deeds for people."

"Ah, a philanthropist?"

"Yes, sir, that's the ticket. He sends us canned food, sir, and very good it is too. Why, I can feel my mouth watering even now, sir. I can't get enough of the stuff. And the charge to His Majesty's Government is very low. He does it out of pure loyalty—and what a good heart he has, Mr. McCracken, even though he's a Papist."

"He's Catholic?"

"Yes, sir. But I wouldn't hold that agin' him. I've known some good fellows next to me in the trenches, sir, that was Catholic. And they're always the best chaplains."

"Why do you think that is?" I asked, hoping to get some reply about solid theology.

"Well, sir, as they doesn't have any family to worry about, they can be braver than our lot, you know."

I didn't like to tell him I was one of those Papists myself, but out of honesty I was about to break the news to him when our conversation was interrupted by the arrival of Sir Timothy LaGrange. At his heels came a man in the uniform of an American Captain.

"Have you boys eaten yet?" LaGrange asked. I couldn't place his accent—English public school, I thought, but with faint strains of somewhere in America, perhaps even some Scots. "Just come back from the Front? Well, tuck in. Thanks for the work you're all doing. There's plenty of food—just help yourself. All canned by my people up in Frithoway! No, don't thank me, I'm just doing my bit."

Nevertheless, I said, "Thank you, Sir Timothy."

LaGrange was already past us, but hearing me he turned and looked closely at me. "Scottish?" he asked. Looking me up and down, he added, "And you're not a regular."

"That's right. My name's McCracken. I'm an engineer, testing the viability of the new Mark V-Star tank."

"McCracken, McCracken." LaGrange repeated the name as if it were an incantation. "I think I've heard of you. An engineer, you say? Well, that's grand. I love engineering! Engineering is the way to win the War, you know. What we need is more machines—tanks, planes, bigger guns. The more machines we have, the quicker we'll beat the Germans."

"If they work right," I said with a bit of a shrug and a grin.

LaGrange's face split in a broad smile. "Haaa-ha. That's very funny. If they work right. Let's just keep the tanks and armoured cars rolling off the factory floors, shall we? We need lots of them—so many the Boche won't know which one to shoot at! Ha ha ha. If they work right. If they work right. Very funny indeed. I do enjoy frank conversations like this."

As he spoke, he was moving away to a new group of soldiers, and the tankers and I picked our way across the lawn to where tin plates were being piled with beef stew. We dropped ourselves onto the grass and tasted it. It was good, though I think my German chef at home, Fritz, might have found a few problems with it.

"I just can't get enough of this beef stew!" rhapsodized Macklethwaite, smacking his lips and holding his plate out for seconds. "I feel like I'm eating as well as a pilot!"

CHAPTER 3
SCHOOLS AND CANNED FOOD

Having reported to D Company HQ, I bade farewell to my tanker companions and, released from service, walked back to the train station. From there, I would ride to Paris, and from Paris catch a plane to London. It was the quickest way of getting back to report to the War Office about the performance of the tank. Going West to LeHavre and catching a boat would take a lot longer, and the U-boats were becoming a menace again, since the Germans had once more lifted their restrictions on torpedoing civilian ships.

The quickest way back to England, I thought with a little bitterness, would be to take an airship, but my own airship was currently in Russia, where my friend Vassily Sikorsky was attempting to rescue his family from the Communist Revolution.

And the train for Paris would not arrive for some hours, so I threw my kitbag down on the platform, rested my head against it, and settled down to try and sleep.

I had just drifted off when an American voice stirred me. I opened my eyes to find an American

Captain, who looked somehow familiar, standing over me.

"Mr. McCracken?" I nodded. "Sorry to disturb you, but Sir Timothy sends his compliments, and would very much like to have a word with you."

That was it! This was the American Captain who had been with Sir Timothy this afternoon. I scrambled to my feet.

"My name is Hanson, Captain Aeneas Hanson."

We shook hands. "Where is Sir Timothy?"

"He's in the station buffet. Says they're often pretty good in France." Captain Hanson pushed open a green door and we went into a large room lit by oil lamps. Several soldiers huddled around tables here and there, together with a few civilians. The smell of the oil mingled with that of fresh bread. Sir Timothy rose from his seat as we approached.

"Mr. McCracken!" he said, thrusting out his hand, which I shook briefly—a dry hand, a perfunctory handshake. "I knew I recognized your name! I knew it! You're the fellow who liberated the Mayan gold for His Majesty's Government, and killed Captain Strombourg, aren't you?"

"Technically, a crocodile killed Captain Strombourg."

Sir Timothy's eye glinted. "Ah, so modest! I like modesty in a man—it's a great virtue. Wouldn't you say so, Father Kerr?" A shadow behind Sir Timothy moved, and out of it emerged a tall Catholic priest with deep-set eyes and a salt-and-pepper beard. We shook hands. "Fr. Kerr is my chaplain—I should say the chaplain of the Frithoway Academy and of my food processing plant. And he's my advisor too, isn't that correct, Fr. Kerr?"

"It is, Sir Timothy," replied Fr. Kerr, gathering the shadows about him once more.

"Sit down, please, McCracken. Would you like some of this excellent bread and cheese? And some coffee? Hanson, see to it, please."

While Hanson poured the coffee, and I pecked at some crusty bread with gruyere, Sir Timothy said, "I thought I recognized you, earlier today. I knew your face from somewhere. It was Fr. Kerr who reminded me of your excellent record. Engineer, isn't that right?" I nodded once more. Hanson placed a cup of coffee in front of me, together with a bowl of sugar and a small pitcher of cream. I fixed my coffee and took a sip. It was superb—only Fritz could make better. "You graduated from Imperial, didn't you? I'm an LSE man myself, but I always thought I should go into engineering. Engineering is the science of today and of tomorrow. You were putting that new version of the Mark V through its paces, weren't you? I thought so. Technology will decide this War in the end, don't you think? And more than that." Sir Timothy leaned forward, clasping his hands earnestly before him. "Technology will decide the future as well—what kind of world we live in."

Suddenly, I saw what I thought he was driving at. "You're a Catholic, aren't you?" I asked.

Sir Timothy's lips broadened into a smile. "Yes, but I hope you won't hold that against me!" He and Hanson laughed, and I joined in a second later, when I realized that he had meant it as a joke. Nothing came from the shadows enveloping Fr. Kerr.

"What I mean," I said, when the laughter had begun to subside, "is that we can use technology for works of mercy. We could use it to feed starving people, to fight against oppressive governments, to educate children . . . "

"That's it!" Sir Timothy pounded the table with his fist, startling me and Hanson, and making the little china plate bearing the bread and cheese jump half an inch in the air. Luckily, I had the coffee in my hand, and only spilt a few drops on my trouser leg. Sir Timothy leaned forward. "That's it," he said again. "Ending hunger and educating the world—that's what it's all about."

Smiling in a self-satisfied way that confused me, he sat back, resting his hands on the arms of his seat. "I do enjoy these frank conversations. It's good for us to be honest with each other, don't you think, Mr. McCracken? Food and education. Those are the two things I'm interested in—two *Catholic* things, as you say." He winked. Standing up, he began to pace back and forth. Orange light from one of the platform lamps flickered across his face as he moved. "Let me tell you a little about myself, Mr. McCracken. I am a very rich man. I made my fortune back in a city in the United States of America called Sioux Falls. Have you heard of it?" I shook my head. "It's not very famous yet, I guess. My father was French, my mother a Scot, like you. They lived in Scotland a while, but when I was a boy, we all emigrated to America. My father left me a small amount of money, which I invested in the railroads." He smiled indulgently. "I supposed you'd say *railways*. I followed one of the lines to Sioux Falls. By this time, I'd made a lot of money, and I wanted to give back." He stopped his pacing a moment and placed his hand upon his chest. "That, I think, is the duty of the wealthy, don't you think, Mr. McCracken? Well, I helped Bishop Marty found the diocese of Sioux Falls, and I put a lot of my money into schools—*Catholic* schools, Mr. McCracken, staffed by

Catholic nuns. Now, I know what you're wondering—there's the education, you're thinking, but where's the technology? Well, let me tell you, Mr. McCracken, Sioux Falls is a meat-packing city. I never put my money in meat, though it's become profitable lately. But I did start to look into the process of canning food. And I came back to Scotland, opening up a factory in the remains of a castle on a tiny island near the Shetlands. My timing was very good— His Majesty's Government was eager to buy canned food for the troops. My new process made it cheaper to can food, so I was able to offer it more cheaply than my competitors. Of course, last year there was all that fuss over the low quality of canned food sent to the Front Line. Not mine—mine was of a very high quality. But I realized there was need of a revolution in the science of food canning. The result was this." Reaching under the table, he tossed me a can, then another, then another. "Roast beef and Yorkshire pudding stew, curried chicken, fried cod—great nutritional value, high quality ingredients, wonderful flavour. Just the thing for boosting the morale of the brave Tommies defending the world against the Kaiser's tyranny."

"Sir Timothy is investigating the possibility of canning hotdogs and hamburgers for the dough-boys shipping from America even now," said Hanson.

Sir Timothy looked a little irritated by the interruption. "I was just coming to that. But anyway, Mr. McCracken, I think you get the picture."

"It's fascinating, and—"

"Yes, I know—thank you, Mr. McCracken, thank you. It's so good to have such an honest conversation! But really, I'm just doing my bit for the war effort. Just doing my bit! And I was wondering—you being the technological sort of fellow you are, pioneer of the portable water turbine, and so forth—I thought you might like to come and see my plant up in Scotland."

"I'd be delighted. Thank—"

"I thought so! Excellent. Mr. McCracken, I *so* appreciate your candour. I feel like I can really talk with you, really get things done. I'll be back in Scotland very shortly. My secretary will contact you with a date. I have a function in Edinburgh before that, which unfortunately I cannot avoid. But after that, I'd love for you to see my operation, and perhaps give me your advice, as you've done this evening. Thank you, Mr. McCracken, thank you very much!"

With this, it was evident that our interview was over, and Captain Hanson was conducting me back to my kitbag. I sat there, still waiting for the Paris train, and reflecting on my bewildering interview with Sir Timothy. I had to admit to myself that I didn't like him. There didn't seem to be anything actually wrong with what he had said, but he was a bore about it. That troubled me, and I prayed for guidance. Nothing came, not even the train.

Finally, it occurred to me that I should not mistrust someone just because he bored me. But that didn't really convince me—something about him did not sit well on my soul. I just couldn't tell what it was.

My train continued to not arrive, and as the night passed, it got colder and colder and I couldn't sleep. In the end, I shrugged off my blanket, got to my feet and started walking up and down the platform, beating my hands against my arms to get them warm, praying the rosary as I went.

As I drew close to the gold-lit window of the buffet, I heard Sir Timothy's voice, and something about its tone compelled me to stop and shrink back against the wall.

"Captain Hanson," Sir Timothy was saying, "the food your government has bought is here; all you need to do is take it."

"But, Sir Timothy," protested Hanson, "that has already been paid for by the British Army. I can't allow my men to take food that's been purchased by someone else. Please, just return the cash we paid for it. We can get food elsewhere, I'm sure."

"Well." Sir Timothy's tone became eminently reasonable. He was a reasonable man talking to another reasonable man who nevertheless had some rather childish scruples. "I suppose that depends somewhat on your point of view. After all, our intention here is to beat the Germans, isn't it? We're all allies, we all want the same thing. The Americans, the British—two armies fighting the same enemy. And sharing is something we all learned to do when we were very small. That's what I'm proposing—that we should share."

There was a short silence, then Hanson spoke. "I wish you'd been able to keep up with production to satisfy both orders."

"Well, there are processes in place that will make sure my people don't ever fall behind like that again. We're at war. We all need to work a little harder, to have faith in our final victory—if only we do our bit first. It's just a question of finding the right incentive, you see." After another silence, Sir Timothy added, "I can see you're being reasonable about this. I do enjoy these sorts of conversation, where we can be perfectly honest with each other. You can't get very far in life being dishonest."

"I feel like I'm being a scoundrel," said Hanson.

"But you're not," answered Sir Timothy. "You're just being reasonable. You're being honest. That's good—those are the best kinds of conversation, the most productive kinds of conversation. And don't worry about the British supplies. I'll make sure . . . "

His voice sank lower, and I couldn't make out anything more. I stood there, shadowed by the window-frame, for a few moments. What was going on? If I understood their conversation correctly, Sir Timothy was trying to get paid twice for the same shipment of food. And our boys were going to lose the food they were expecting.

I stole silently away from the train platform, and searched through the dark streets. It wasn't easy to find my way, because of the blackout, but in the end I found D Company HQ, where I had earlier debriefed after the tank evaluation. A chink of light showed around one blackout screen, I saw, as I climbed the steps. The private on guard duty looked at my identification papers, holding them up to the scanty light, then waved me inside. An adjutant I'd met before, named Ashe, who was passing from one room to another with a sheaf of papers recognized me.

"Hello, McCracken. I thought you'd be in Paris by now." He paused while a dull thud shook the light fixtures. "Uh-oh," he said. "They've started again."

"May I see Captain Dowling?" I asked. "It's an urgent matter."

Ashe raised an eyebrow. "Certainly—I'll see if he's free." His disappeared through a door, leaving me in the hallway. People passed back and forth, mainly officers, but some nurses and enlisted men. At length, Ashe peered round the door. "Step this way, McCracken," he said.

Captain Dowling, his peaked cap removed to reveal his thinning hair, stood behind a table with other officers grouped around him. He looked up from the map they were all studying.

"Well, what is it, McCracken? I'm afraid I'm a bit busy at the moment."

I quickly explained what I had overheard. "I thought that might be important," I concluded.

"Of course it's important. Armchair generals talk about strategy; real generals talk about supply. And it sounds as if this friend of yours is messing with my supplies." Dowling smacked the palm of his hand with his riding crop. "The bounder! Does he have no sense of decency, no sense of loyalty?" Turning to the adjutant, he said, "Ashe, why don't you take four or five privates and set a guard about the storeroom?"

Ashe snapped to the salute, and the two of us exited rapidly while the officers went back to their war conference. The house shook as a German shell exploded nearby.

"Four years of stalemate," remarked Ashe, "until now. This is the furthest the Hun has penetrated since the very beginning of the War." Another explosion, and the windows rattled. Several voices around us gasped. Ashe pointed at a private and gave a few brisk orders. A moment later, he and I were striding through the darkness, half a dozen soldiers marching behind us.

"Sir!" cried one of the soldiers, pointing. "Gotha!"

"Take cover!" shouted Ashe.

I dashed off a quick Hail Mary as we scattered. Flattening myself on the ground, I twisted my neck to look up. A huge shadow blacked out the stars ahead of us: the wide double wings of a Gotha, a large aeroplane used by the Germans for bombing. As I watched, an explosion shook the ground. Before the light of the first explosion died, another churned up the street ahead of us, and another. The near explosion lifted me bodily into the air; for a moment, I think I must have lost consciousness, because the next thing I knew, I was on my back and a couple of yards away from where I had lain down. My brain was whirling, and my ears rang as if there were church bells in them. Greasy black smoke drifted across the street, and the stench of burned powder hung heavily on the air. Ashe picked himself up, ghostlike in his covering of pale dust. A dot of bright red blood beneath one nostril gave the single colour to his appearance.

I climbed shakily to my feet, making the Sign of the Cross. "Were you hit?" I asked.

Ashe shook his head, looking a little dazed. "Spot of concussion, that's all, I think. That was a close one!"

Silence had settled over the street, except for the drone of the Gotha's engines as it rose away from its bombing run and turned for home. We quickly reassembled and resumed our march; God be praised, but no one had been hurt. We picked our way between smoking craters. A building off to our left was on fire, and already a bucket-chain had formed, civilians rubbing shoulders with British and French soldiers.

At last we reached the small storage depot. Eight Ford trucks had pulled up in front of it. Some of them bore red crosses. The rearmost truck had its bonnet open, and the mechanic was peering at the engine while the driver looked on.

"Yes, it's Tin, Tin, Tin," chanted the driver merrily.

> "You exasperating puzzle, Hunk o' Tin.
> I've abused you and I've flayed you,
> But by Henry Ford who made you,
> You are better than a Packard,
> >   Hunk o' Tin."

His rhyme brought out a chorus of laughter from those assembled round about. Meanwhile, several American soldiers were emerging from the depot, carrying large crates marked LAGRANGE CANNED FOODS, LTD., FRITH, SCOTLAND. With them came Hanson and Sir Timothy.

"Wait right there!" cried Ashe, holding out his swagger stick and dashing forward. "You can't take those. They belong to His Britannic Majesty's Army."

Sir Timothy turned to Hanson. "I thought these were the crates *your* government purchased, Captain."

Captain Hanson's mouth opened and closed several times, like a fish on dry land. I thought a saw a quiver pass through his frame, and his face blushed. I felt sorry for him.

Ashe reached into his attaché case and flourished a sheaf of papers. "Here is the receipt for this purchase, sir. I'm afraid you must have made a mistake." He held them out to Hanson.

Hanson gave a weak smile. "No need to look at the receipt, Lieutenant," he said. "I trust all is in order. It's I who have made the mistake." Rounding on Sir Timothy, he snapped, "Where do you think those crates could be, Sir Timothy?"

Sir Timothy spread his hands. "If they're not here in the city, they're most likely in transit. When I get back to Scotland, I'll see what I can find out and cable you."

Hanson turned back to Ashe. "Sorry for the inconvenience, Lieutenant. Men, put those crates back where you got them. It seems they're not ours." It might have been my imagination, but I think I caught a glimpse of anger in his eye as he glanced at Sir Timothy.

"Good evening, McCracken." Sir Timothy had fixed me with his eye. "How odd to see you here. I thought you'd be on your way to Paris by now."

"The train was late, Sir Timothy," I answered. "But I'm glad to see you again."

"Yes, a fortunate happenstance. Perhaps we shall meet again, soon. At any rate, you'll be visiting me at my plant up on Frith, won't you? Of course you will. I look forward to renewing our acquaintance. I do so love our conversations. I appreciate the honesty we both find in them."

"So do I, Sir Timothy," I replied, "so do I."

CHAPTER 4
IN THE STUDY

Ariadne McCracken, the dark-haired American beauty who had generously consented to marry me five years previously, sat on the other side of the coal fire from me in the study of our little flat in London, which we had rented since our return from Asia just before Christmas. Archie, our two-year-old son, was attempting to build walls around our cat, Edison, who kept foiling his plans by climbing over them and moving to other warm places. The wind rattled the windows—as the first day of April drew to a close, it showed as yet no promise of summer.

"So," said Ari, putting aside her book on the Caribbean Creoles, "how was the War Secretary?"

Pulling off my boots, I stretched my toes out towards the fire that leaped and danced in the grate. "About what you'd expect," I said. "He wouldn't tell me what he was going to do about the Mark V. They never do. Did you see the zeppelin?" During my conference with the War Secretary at the Legionnaires Club on King Charles Street, there had been an air raid that had shattered one of the windows. No one was hurt—the blackout screen caught most of the shards of glass.

"We heard the maroons," Ari told me, referring to the fireworks by which the Fire Brigade informed London's citizens that an air raid was about to begin, "but it didn't come close. It reminded me of the LS3." She gave me a nostalgic smile.

"It's those Mercedes engines." Parting the blackout curtain, I looked out over the darkened city. Raindrops drew wiggly lines down the windowpane. Sighing, I said, "It doesn't seem as if this War will ever end."

"Almost four years," Ari mused. She winced, placing a hand on her tummy.

"Are you all right?" I asked, hurrying to her side. "Can I get you anything?"

"I'm fine. But the baby's kicking."

The door opened, and our German servant, Fritz, entered. Wall-eyed and with wild red hair, Fritz was the best chef I'd ever met, and a crack shot with a side-arm.

"Herr Archimedes," he said, "it is time that to bed you must retire."

"Archie," said Ari, when Archie made a study of pretending to not have heard Fritz, "it's time for bed."

Still nothing from Archie. I strode over and picked up the now-wriggling child, handing him to Fritz. "Time for bed, Archie," I said. Tracing the Sign of the Cross on his forehead, I gave Archie a night blessing. Archie was still for the blessing, but resumed squirming as Fritz carried him through the door. We could still hear his "No no no no no *no-o-o-o!*" fading as Fritz carried him to his bedroom.

"Honey?" I spun round at Ari's word. "You seem to be lost in thought."

I passed a hand through my hair. "I was just thinking about the poor boys in the trench. It's a wonder, isn't it? I mean, why did I survive, and they didn't?"

Ari got up, pulled my chin down and kissed me lightly. "I was praying for you the whole time you were away, you know."

I nodded. "I know that. But those boys had mothers and girlfriends who were praying for them too. Why did God—"

Ari put her slender forefinger over my lips. "Shh. Our Lord is in charge. We just have to remain firm in our faith. Only He can sort it all out."

"But on that scale? Sweetheart, it was so large. I couldn't see the ends of No-Man's Land. They say it stretches from the Channel all the way south to Switzerland. And they're dying all along it. Isn't that enough? Aren't we finished yet?"

Ari searched behind my eyes, and there was a deep sadness in hers. "Hold me," she said, and I pulled her close. We stood like that for a long time, until she asked, "How did you celebrate your birthday at the Front?"

I gave a small start. "It was my birthday? What day is it now?" I glanced at the newspaper. Monday, April 1st.

"Your birthday was Friday," Ari explained.

"How old was I?"

"It was a big one. It had a zero at the end."

I scratched my head. "I don't think I'm fifty yet," I reasoned, "and I think I remember Thirty. That doesn't leave much to be guessed at." I narrowed my eyes at her. "How old are you?"

She narrowed her eyes back, wrinkling her delightful nose. "I've already told you. You don't want me to repeat myself, do you? Anyway, a gentleman doesn't ask such questions of a lady." Kissing me, she returned to her seat. "Even if he's married to her. Oh, I forgot." Reaching down beside her chair, she picked up an envelope and handed it to me. "This came for you."

It was postmarked Aberdeen, the city of my birth. Tearing it open, I scanned the lines of print inside. "It's an invitation."

"A birthday party?" Ari was confused.

"No, a Gathering, a reconciliation."

"Between whom?"

"The McCrackens and the McNaughtons," I said. Ari's eyebrows contracted slightly, so I explained: "The McCrackens and the McNaughtons have been feuding for three hundred years. It was all about a stolen lover, a dead blackbird, and a snipe hunt."

"A snipe hunt?"

I lowered the paper in consternation. "There's no such thing as a snipe," I lamented. "The McNaughtons are the Presbyterian branch of the family—we became Catholics to spite them after the incident with the blackbird."

"What incident with the blackbird?"

"Och, it disnae bear the tellin', wooman!" I retorted.

Ari cocked her head disapprovingly at me. "You must be agitated—you've slipped into Scots."

"Sorry. There'll be another time for the story. We can't go, of course. The Daimler is in Russia. We could catch the train, but that's expensive—coal rationing and all. I know your family has money, but it's all in America."

"That's a shame," said Ari glumly. "It would be nice to meet your folks."

At that moment, Fritz returned with a pot of tea and cups on a trolley, and the conversation turned elsewhere.

* * *

I was awoken the following morning by tiny, cold fingers prying my eyelids apart. Archie's face went in and out of focus a few times.

"Daddy, there a man down'tairs."

"Does he want me?" Archie gave an earnest nod. "What time is it?"

Archie's brow furrowed and he wrinkled his nose in a way just like his mother. "Daddy, I can't tell time." With both hands, he twisted my head almost off so I could see the clock. It was about seven o'clock.

"Thank you, dear. Tell the man I'll be right down."

A few minutes later, hastily dressed, my teeth brushed but my chin unshaven, I reached the foot of the stairs, where I was intercepted by Fritz.

"I apologize, Herr McCracken," he said in a hurried whisper. "This man, how he gets in I do not know. I think Master Archie is letting him in."

"Archie can't open the door yet. Don't worry about it, Fritz, but stay close."

I entered the study, to find there a man in a dark overcoat, a kind of shapeless bag in one hand. He was standing with his back to me, examining the books on our shelf, and he didn't turn round to speak. "Good morning, Mac. How have you been?"

I paused, rubbing my sore neck. "I'm sorry. With whom have I the pleasure of speaking?"

"Someone," he said, "you used to know well. I hope you don't mind, but I let myself in and sent your son up to get you."

I didn't know how to respond. There was something sinister here. Did I recognize the voice? What was going on? "You let yourself in?"

"Don't you remember, all those years ago?" he asked, still without turning round. Then, against all my expectations, he began to sing: "We are, we are, we are, we are, we are the engineers!"

I gasped, then sang on: "We can, we can, we can, we can demolish forty beers." The man turned round, smiling broadly. It was, as the song indicated, an old friend from college. "Johnnie Birrell!" I cried, clasping his hand warmly. "How have you been?" His reddish hair was paler and thinner than I remembered, and he was heavier-set than he had been, but the handshake was firm, his hand muscular, not soft. "Has it really been twenty years, Birrell?"

Birrell shrugged. "Well, eighteen."

"Close enough for government work, eh?" I motioned him into the wing chair in which Ari had been sitting on the previous night.

"It's funny you should mention that, old chap." Birrell plopped the bag down on the table between us, and a faint earthy smell puffed up from it in an invisible cloud. "Potatoes," he announced. "Know a man who grows them."

I called Fritz in, and his eyes lit up—we hadn't seen potatoes in several weeks. They had been pretty scarce for a while in England. He took them, with promises to make something delicious out of them as he hurried from the room.

"What have you been up to, Birrell?" I asked, when the door had clicked behind Fritz.

Birrell sat back in the wing chair and crossed his legs. "Well, after graduation, went to the Punjab to dig canals for Her Imperial Majesty. You may have heard, there was some unrest there before the War—Muslims wanting their own Indian state, stuff like that. Then there was a bill before Parliament that attempted to confiscate the property of Punjabi who died without heirs. That led to a riot, and yours truly was involved in putting that down. Someone in Whitehall heard what I'd done, and before I knew it, I was recruited into an exciting new government department."

"Fascinating," I said encouragingly.

Birrell gave a nod. "Thank you. Approached by a chap called . . . well, whom we call C, who was starting an organization called the Secret Service Bureau."

"Secret Service Bureau!" I exclaimed. "Birrell, are you a spy?"

Birrell gave a short laugh. "Steady on, old chap. Even if I were, I couldn't exactly tell you, could I? It's really nothing romantic at all—we're just government plodders, who occasionally go off solving problems in foreign parts. It mostly involves counting train carriages and creeping around naval dockyards."

Before we could say any more, the door opened, and we both rose to greet Ari. She wore a long, flowing red dress with a white collar. You could barely even guess yet at the baby on the way.

"I say, old chap, congratulations!" cried Birrell. "Congratulations, both of you. When will the little chap be arriving?"

"August," said Ari, lowering herself into the chair I pulled up for her. "Archie is around here somewhere—he's our eldest."

"Well!" said Birrell. "I go away for a few years, and it seems everyone goes and starts a family! I suppose I'd better catch up soon."

"You're not married, Mr. Birrell?" asked Ari.

The vaguest hint of a shadow passed over Birrell's face. "Thought about it once. Poor girl bought it shortly before the War. Can't say I've ever really got over it—unfair to marry a girl with that on my soul." He flashed us each a smile. "Still, does no good dwelling on past events. Not past marrying age yet, am I? But I was going to tell you about some business this Bureau of mine has got its nose into. A chap who will interest you a great deal: Sir Timothy LaGrange."

"LaGrange! I met him just a few days ago."

Simultaneously, Ari cried out, "You met Sir Timothy LaGrange and didn't tell me!" and Birrell said quietly, "Yes, we know." Having said that, he turned to Ari and asked, "What do you know about Sir Timothy, Mrs. McCracken?"

Ari settled herself comfortably in her armchair. The door opened, and Fritz wheeled in the tea-cart bearing a coffee pot, cups, saucers, spoons, a creamer, a sugar bowl, and a plate of biscuits. Virtually the only dissension between Ari and Fritz was her insistence on calling them *cookies* instead of *biscuits*. Fritz poured, then left us alone again.

"All I know about Sir Timothy is that he's a Catholic philanthropist. He's provided food for troops at the Front, and he's an educator—he runs some kind of experimental school in Scotland somewhere."

"The Isle of Frith," I added to her tale. "It's near the Shetlands."

Leaning a little closer to Birrell, Ari said, "This is a Catholic family, Mr. Birrell. There's quite a prejudice against us in this country. So it's wonderful that Sir Timothy is helping dispel the myth that all Catholics are evil and superstitious."

Birrell pressed his fingertips together. "I completely sympathize, Mrs. McCracken. My mother was Catholic also. Perhaps, after the War, we can all forget our pre-War prejudices. Until then, I believe you're quite correct. However, something about Sir Timothy doesn't quite add up."

I thought about Sir Timothy's attempt to get paid twice for the same shipment of food, but didn't want to mention it; after all, there is such a sin as detraction.

"Here's something else you might not know, McCracken. Sir Timothy is a McNaughton."

"Is he now!" My scruples against detraction were beginning to crumble.

"His mother was the McNaughton; his father was French, from Picardy, and he emigrated to America to make his fortune."

"He told me about that," I said, and related to them what Sir Timothy had told me.

Birrell nodded. "Well, that more or less agrees with what we know about him." He paused, and shifted uncomfortably in his seat. "Now, this is personal, McCracken. There are two things about Sir Timothy. One is a discrepancy, the other something I can't prove. Together, they add up to a great deal of suspicion on my part, but nothing I can send a man to jail for. The discrepancy is that Sir Timothy's net worth in 1894, when he left America, was about a million dollars. Quite a comfortable sum. When he arrived back in Scotland, in 1912, he was worth about twenty times that."

I gave a long whistle. "Where was he all that time? I must visit the place."

"Frankly, old chap, nobody really knows where Sir Timothy was all that time—almost twenty years! Is the Sir Timothy whose picture is so frequently on the front page of the *Times* even the same Tim LaGrange who made his million renting corral space in the Dakotas? Nobody can tell for sure."

"Well, that's the discrepancy," said Ari. "What is it you can't prove?"

"It's an eyewitness testimony, Mrs. McCracken," Birrell said, still squirming slightly. "My own. You see, when C formed the Secret Service Bureau back in '09, he posted me to Berlin. Our whole purpose in those days was to keep an eye on the Imperial German Government, to try and find out what they were up to." He gave an ironic snort. "I suppose we all know now. Anyway, as part of my assignment, I went to a ball at the City Palace in Berlin. And there I saw Sir Timothy LaGrange—I'm sure it was he—in most earnest conversation with the Kaiser."

Chapter 5
The Flying Scotsman

Silence stretched out between us in the little study. I could hear the clock ticking in the hall, Archie's voice singing, the noises outside the window—the hum of people, the engines and horns of omnibuses, the occasional whinny of a horse. But all was still in here, as if time had stopped. It was like a little still world in the midst of normal life.

I knew an adventure was about to begin.

"What can we do about all this, Birrell?" I asked.

"Glad you asked that, old chap," answered Birrell. "You know, I'm the agent, I've got the official position. But you're the one who's had all the adventures. We have a file an inch thick on you at the Bureau, you know. Nobody doubts your loyalty, of course, even though your servant, his wife, and his fourteen children are all from Bavaria." I must have frowned at this—it sounded almost like a threat. Birrell hurried to add: "Please don't get me wrong, old chap—we know of Mr. Bauer's loyalty too. In fact, his wife is one of our informants in Bavaria. Some of their children too, I think—we've received some very interesting sketches of U-boat technology from one of Mr. Bauer's sons. Anyway, point is that my career, beside yours, has been positively pedestrian. What we'd like you to do, if you're willing, is to snoop around Sir Timothy and just tell us what you find. What is he up to? Does he have a real connection with Kaiser Bill? How did he make his fortune—is he sponsored by the Hun? There's no crime in having talked to Kaiser Bill before the War started. I might be wrong about Sir Timothy; or I might not. I'm hoping you can confirm my fears, or put them to rest."

A little suspicion lingered in me. "Do I have a choice?"

Birrell blinked. "Why, of course you do, old chap. We can't force you to do this. A forced man makes a bad agent."

"Oh."

"Especially because this is all based on a hunch, not on facts. But I do hope you'll say yes, old chap."

"Where would I begin?"

Birrell became businesslike. "You've probably already received the invitation to the Gathering in Edinburgh—the reconciliation between the McNaughtons and the McCrackens?"

"We can't get there," put in Ari. "Coal rationing—train tickets are expensive."

Birrell reached into his breast pockets and drew out some small pieces of paper. "Tickets for the Flying Scotsman to Edinburgh, with a connecting train two days later to Aberdeen and a ferry to Lerwick in the Shetlands. Will you do it, McCracken?" He leaned forward hopefully.

My eyes slid over to Ari. "Only if I can take my family with me," I said firmly.

Birrell's smile spread across his face. He took out more tickets and placed them on the table. "I thought I ought to try to persuade you not to," he said, "but I knew I wouldn't be able to dissuade you from doing so."

Ari smiled. "Adventuring is our family business," she said.

* * *

A little before ten o'clock the following morning, after a breakfast of German potato cakes made with relish by Fritz, a taxi dropped us off at the entrance to King's Cross Station, Fritz beckoning to a porter to help with our luggage. As the porter loaded up a cart, I looked across the road at the motley collection of shops that was colloquially called the African Village and wondered why. None of the African villages I'd seen resembled it even closely.

My eyes clicked with a man in a boater, leaning against a corner and reading a newspaper. Catching my glance, he instantly looked away and began to fold the newspaper. A ragman's cart trundled along the street between us, and when it had passed, he was gone.

"Mac?" I shook myself and turned my attention to Ari. She never looked so beautiful to me as when she was expecting one of our children, and I leaned forward to kiss her on the lips. "Mac, will you take Archie, please?"

"Of course." Archie's hand slipped into mine. "A busy train station like this is part of a young gentleman's education."

Passing through the turnstile we found ourselves in the glass-roofed tunnel that comprised platforms 1 and 2 of King's Cross. The Flying Scotsman was already waiting, its smart green paint gleaming in the morning sunlight, wreathed in magical steam.

"See that, Archie?" He looked up at the huge mechanical muscle that was going to haul us almost the entire length of England and Scotland in a day. "That's a GNR Class 1 4-4-2 locomotive engine, that is, designed by Henry Ivatt and built at the Doncaster—"

"Daddy," said Archie, his eyebrows raised quizzically as he looked up at me, "it's a train."

"No, no. Technically, the train is the whole vehicle, including the tender and carriages. See." I pointed at the polished wood of the carriages behind the locomotive's tender. "Those are the carriages, that's the locomotive, and this is the tender. It carries coal."

Archie's raised eyebrows told me unambiguously that I was crazy. "Actually, Daddy, it's a train," he said, from the full height of his scorn at my intellectual limitations.

"But the train is the whole thing. Mummy, will you tell him? Daddy knows what he's talking about. He has a degree from Imperial College."

"It's a train, Daddy." Archie's pursed lips conveyed how distasteful further debate would be on this topic, so I gave up.

We wove in and out among the excited bustle that was all around us, people embarking on exciting journeys to far-flung places, ladies in fur coats and wide-brimmed hats, gentlemen in top-hats who were trying not to look as if they knew exactly what train they were catching and when it departed, children of all ages squealing with delight at the coming journey. Not far away, two gentlemen dressed like butlers loaded victuals into the dining carriage. Coal rationing had reduced the number of departures, but the platforms still crowded in the same old way.

It didn't take long for the porter to locate our carriage. We had a compartment to ourselves, two ranks of plush seats facing each other, with windows on either side. Through one set of windows, we could see the crowds on the platform; through the other, the passageway that ran the whole length of the carriage.

I caught Ari smiling at me. "What?" I asked.

"You," she said. "Your eyes always shine so at the beginning of a train journey."

"Or a ship journey, or a zeppelin journey, or a flight in a plane." I grinned wider. "Mechanized transport. It's the way of the future!" I paused and frowned. "Och, I sound like Sir Timothy LaGrange."

"Well," said Ari, settling herself back in her seat and unpinning her hat, "I do hope we're wrong about him."

A fountain of steam erupted from the engine, and with a lurch the Flying Scotsman started moving along the platform. We moved at first through cityscapes, then through the rows of brick houses and parks that made up London's suburbs, then out into the countryside. At first, Archie was content to press his nose against the window, watch the telegraph poles flit past, and maintain a constant narrative on what he could see, which included cows, trees, motor-cars and other objects of less significance. But in the end, he got restless and I took him for a walk.

The Flying Scotsman is one of the fastest trains in Britain, but also one of the most luxurious. The dining carriage, for example, looked like a long, narrow five-star restaurant, the waiters all dressed like my Aunt Polly's butler in starched collars and tails. We explored up to the front coach, and found a window through which we could see the tender. I tried the handle, but the door was locked.

"Sorry, Sproggin," I said. "We can't get to the engine like that. Let's wait till we get to York and we can have a quick look then. Perhaps the engineer will let us ride with him for a few miles, eh?"

I suddenly got one of those feelings you get when you're being watched, and turned my head to look behind me. The door to the toilet was just closing. I shook my head a few times and went with Archie to complete our exploration.

"Come and sit with Mommy," said Ari to Archie upon our return. "It's time for you to take a little nap." He sat with her but wriggled a lot.

"He probably wants to play a bit more," I said.

"It's his nap time, and he should go to sleep, even if it's only for a short time," returned Ari. "Honey, would you go to the dining car and get me something to drink?"

"Champagne cocktail?" I wondered.

She shook her head. "A glass of water will be fine for now."

"Where's Fritz?"

"Restroom, I think." She frowned. "Is something wrong?"

I shrugged. "I just can't shake the feeling that we're being followed. I saw someone outside the station who seemed to be watching us, and I could feel someone watching me just now when I was exploring with Archie."

"Perhaps Sir Timothy is keeping an eye on you," said Ari. "Or perhaps it was Johnnie."

I shook my head. "Birrell knows where I'm going. Why would he follow me? It was probably my imagination," I concluded, rising from my seat.

Back in the dining coach, people were beginning to gather for lunch, and I had to squeeze through something of a press to reach the bar. I looked along it to find an empty seat, and as I did so, my blood froze. It was like seeing somebody you thought was dead.

For a moment, I couldn't budge an inch. Then I moved over to the bar and waited for the bar-tender to notice me. He was busy, and I was in no hurry. My eyes darted back and forth along the bar, and I moved forward, leaning on it between two seated people. I put my mouth as close as I could to the ear of one of them and said, "Herr Damlich, I wish I could say it was nice to see you. I thought you were dead."

This old acquaintance of mine, who was a German saboteur and spy, looked up at me, and I thought I saw shock and surprise transform his face for a brief moment. "McCracken?" he said.

The young man sitting next to Damlich saw that we were acquaintances, and with a smile rose to let me sit down. Thanking him, I took his seat. I ran my eye over Damlich, noting that the bulge in his left jacket pocket was almost certainly a Luger.

"I thought you were dead, Damlich," I said again. "The last time I saw you, Fritz had plugged you and you were falling off a New York wharf."

"A shoulder wound is not totally debilitating, Herr McCracken," Damlich whispered back with a snarl, "though I was in recovering several months."

I gave a narrow smile. "I just can't get rid of you. I throw you off a train in Canada, Fritz shoots you off a dock in New York City, and you just won't go away. So what are you here for?" My visual inspection took in also the carpet bag at Damlich's feet. "What's in the bag, Damlich?" I leaned a little closer, dropping my voice. "Is it a bomb?"

"You could open it and find out," replied the spy.

"Perhaps I'll let the Transport Police do that. They shoot spies, you know."

Damlich shook his head. "I cannot allow that, Herr McCracken, as you are aware."

"Perhaps you won't have much choice—take your hand away from your gun. Do you think I'm unarmed?"

"I would never assume that, Herr McCracken," answered Damlich, placing his hands on the bar.

Actually, I was unarmed, but I didn't want him to know that. I said, "Get up, pick up your bag, and walk out of the carriage. Remember, I'm behind you."

"To forget that would be hard."

We started to move out of the carriage. My eyes were fixed on the bag, which I was convinced contained a bomb. About halfway to the door, Damlich had to squeeze round a waiter with a tea cart. As soon as he was on the other side of the waiter, he snatched a quick glance back at me, stooped, and dashed for the door.

I caught my breath—not having a gun on me, I couldn't do much. The door opened and closed, with Damlich on the other side. I ran up to the door and wrenched it open.

I found myself in the cold little room that every coach had at the end, with the moving floor in the middle where the coaches were joined. But

I saw none of this—I just saw the butt of the Luger descending towards my head.

Then I blacked out.

Chapter 6
Welcome to Scotland

I was awoken by a blast of freezing air, and found myself halfway through the open door of the train carriage, Damlich on top of me and shoving me out into the speed-blurred countryside through which the Flying Scotsman rocketed. Seeing that I had awoken, he paused in his labours.

"You see, Herr McCracken?" Damlich had to yell—the wind roared past the open doorway like a thunderstorm. "You throw me off a train in Canada, and I throw you off a train in England. It is—how you say?—stops."

He meant *quits*, but I didn't want to correct his vocabulary with my head hanging out of a train.

Damlich began shoving once more, but this time I resisted. It was hard, because my head spun and throbbed with pain.

Suddenly, there came a scream. A couple of passengers had emerged from the dining car and seen the fight. Damlich spun around in surprise, and this gave me the moment I needed to thrust my knee up into the soft flesh of his stomach. With a grunt, he doubled up and released me.

Reaching up, I grabbed him by the front of his jacket and heaved him off me. In moments, we were grappling in the open doorway, the ends of the sleepers flashing by beneath us, the carriage filling up with smoke from the engine.

One hefty push, and Damlich fell backwards through the open door. But he caught hold of a brass rail. For a moment, his feet flew back, and it looked as if he would tumble from the train. But he managed to gain control of himself and clung onto the side of the carriage.

I quickly took in my surroundings. Damlich had left the carpet-bag, but there was no sign of his Luger, so he must still have that with him. God bless him, Fritz had turned up, and his Mauser C96 was in his hand. Fritz assessed the situation in a second and stepped into the doorway to fire at Damlich. But the German was gone.

Fritz and I looked at each other in a moment of confusion. He must have climbed onto the roof of the carriage, I concluded. Cupping my hand about Fritz's ear, I said quietly, so as not to cause a panic among the passengers who were watching, "Check the carpet-bag—it may contain a bomb."

Fritz nodded and I swung myself out and onto the side of the coach.

A railing at the edge of the roof ran all the way along the coach, and I could see Damlich picking his way between the ventilators of the next coach forward. I grabbed the railing and heaved myself up onto the roof. I crawled a yard and then cautiously got to my feet. The coach rattled and swayed beneath my feet, the wind flattened my clothes and felt as if it would blow me off at any moment. A gunshot rang out and the bullet sent up a spark from the roof just an inch from my feet.

I hadn't thought to ask Fritz for his Mauser.

The realization dawned on Damlich that I was unarmed, and a grin spread across his face. He walked slowly towards me, the Luger extended, adjusting his weight as the train swayed this way and that.

"Now," said Damlich, "please to sit down, Herr McCracken." The cold wind froze my body as I slowly lowered myself onto the roof in a sitting position. He smiled. "This seems a familiar situation to me, Herr McCracken. Where could I have seen this before? Perhaps in Canada, I think?"

I said nothing. The wind was terrifically powerful and freezing cold, and I was in no mood to banter with an idiot spy.

Damlich became suddenly serious. "I wish to correct you on a trifling matter, Herr

McCracken," he said. "You should know that I am a saboteur, but also I can enemies interrogate and like an assassin kill men. I am very versatile."

"Nevertheless," I shouted back, "I bet you're better at one of those things than the others."

"We shall see," replied Damlich with a smirk. "Shall we see, for example, how good I am at killing men?" He straightened his arm. The Luger's muzzle stared with dark stupidity at me. Damlich's finger tensed on the trigger, a faint smile playing about his lips.

"Shall we at least wait till the other side of the tunnel?" I inquired.

"Really, Herr McCracken," he answered, "such a bluff of you is unworthy." The Luger's muzzle trained itself between my eyes. But then Damlich thought again, and glanced over his shoulder. "*Gott im Himmel!*" he shouted, and dropped to his knees.

A moment later, the train plunged into the mouth of a tunnel, whistling like a banshee, the sound amplified to a deafening quality by the close confines. I flattened myself against the roof of the coach, while the wind tugged and pulled at me. All about me was a darkness more intense than I could remember—so dark I could almost feel it. And yet the air was full of sparks flying back from the locomotive, like living stars dancing all about me but giving no illumination. And it was freezing, clammy and cold and full of pungent smoke that cloyed in my lungs and made me choke. I fought to keep my wits about me: when we emerged from the tunnel, I would need to be thinking straight.

Ahead of us, I saw a tiny blue light, which grew rapidly. I had to blink over and over, for the smoke made my eyes smart.

And then we were in the open air again, the wind howling about us. Damlich was crouched ahead of me, his Luger still in his hand.

Summoning all my nerve to ignore the possible consequences, I launched myself forward at him. He swung the Luger round towards me, but his aim was off, and though the muzzle flashed with sharp anger, the bullet went wide. My outstretched hands struck him on the shoulders, and he pitched over backwards, with me on top of him.

But I was out of control, and the motion of the train rolled me off him. I continued to roll, sliding off the edge of the roof. My hand flailed out, and caught something cold and metallic. I curled my fingers about it and clung onto it for life. For a few seconds, my legs thrashed in mid-air, while the icy wind roared about me. I reached up with my other hand, and seized hold of the guard-rail that ran along the top of the roof. In a few moments, I thought, I would be back on the roof.

But then Damlich's face appeared above me. The Luger rose towards me, inches from my forehead.

"This is quite an experience, *ja*?" said Damlich. "Very different from last time. This time, I think, the one to get off the train early will be you." Once again, his finger tensed on the trigger.

But he didn't squeeze it. For a split second, his eyes widened in fear, and then, inexplicably, he was gone. A few seconds passed, and then some hands seized me by the wrists and pulled. My feet scrambled on the side of the coach, and then, released, I sprawled on the roof of the carriage, my eyes flashing this way and that to see who my saviour was.

Above me, his legs straddled and his arms akimbo, was a figure of short stature, his ginger hair waving in the wind.

"Fritz!" I cried. "Thank God you're here!"

"Let us go, Herr McCracken," replied Fritz, pulling me to my feet. We both made our way back to the open door and swung ourselves back into safety. "The bag I check," Fritz explained, "but no bomb can I find. So I think, 'Herr McCracken, he needs my help.' So I go up to help."

The carpet-bag was open. It contained clothing, some wads of money, and a small black book that Fritz identified as a German code book. No bomb.

After that, we had a lot of explaining to do to the Transport Police. But a cable to the War Office sorted it out, and before long all was back to normal on the Flying Scotsman. We were not much late arriving in Edinburgh, and we stepped down onto the platform at nearly eight o'clock.

"Do ye smell that?" I asked, drawing in a deep breath.

Ari's nose wrinkled. "Do you mean the coal, the oil, and the smoke? It smells like a train to me."

I frowned at her. "Sniff again," I advised. "Can ye no smell the sun on the heather? The blood of my ancestors on the hillside? Do ye no hear the skirl of the bagpipes echoing along the loch? It's Scotland!"

"You know, your accent is getting stronger." Ari took Archie by the hand. "Soon, we'll have a whole new language to learn!" Archie nodded and wiped his nose on Ari's skirt.

Fritz hurried up to us to tell us that he had found a taxi, and for a few minutes we loaded our luggage. The taxi took us, jolting over the cobblestones, to our hotel, a charming little inn of grey stone that had greenery climbing over the walls, speckled with tiny red flowers.

"Azaleas!" I cried in surprise.

"When did you become a botanist?" asked Ari, equally surprised.

I pointed as we paused outside the door. "The trailing azalea proper." Passing a hand over my brow, I glanced up at the coat of arms carved into the lintel. Sure enough, although it was partly obscured by the azaleas, there was no mistaking the stone tower, wrapped about by a ribbon or belt, upon which was written SPERO IN DEO. "I hope in God?" Ari nodded, her brow deeply furrowed. "Fritz, are you sure this is the right place?"

Fritz dug in his jacket pocket and drew out a piece of paper upon which he had scrawled the address of the inn at which he had booked our rooms. "*Jawohl*, Herr McCracken. This is the place which Herr Birrell gave to me the address."

"Clan McNaughton." In a whisper, I added to Ari, "This inn is a Clan McNaughton place."

Archie squirmed in Ari's arms and, narrowing her eyes in disapproval and warning, she pushed open the door and forged ahead of me. Inside was warm. The walls, paneled in deep mahogany, bore the portraits of claymore-wielding and tartan-wearing ancestors of the McNaughton clan. A little lady with a grey bun fixed tightly to the back of her head stood behind the counter.

"Now, will you be Mr. McCracken?" she asked, carefully opening the guest book and running her finger down the entries.

"Aye," I replied. "My man booked us two rooms a few days ago."

"From . . . *London*." Her lip curled with disapproval. She fixed me with one bright, rather terrifying eye. "My name is Mary McNaughton. Nae doubt you've heard the family name before?"

"I have, and I'm pleased to meet you."

"And I you, Mr. *McCracken*." She shook my hand with frigidity. "Will you be up here for the snipe hunting, then?"

"Och, but ye ken I'll not be," I answered. "Nae more than ye'll be after shootin' a blackbird."

Mrs. McNaughton leaned across the counter. "There's a papist kirk in town," she explained with venom, "if ye'll be wantin' to pray to yer statues and yer wooden beads like heathens."

"Well, Mrs. McNaughton," I said, my wrinkled nose inches from hers, "at least I'll be able to find a tolerable conversation about the Almighty and the Guid Buik there, rather than all yer heretical reformist nonsense."

Mrs. McNaughton looked as if she was considering a welter of venomous replies, but contented herself with, "Will ye be stayin' twa nichts, or jist ane?"

"Twa nichts, Mrs. McNaughton," I answered.

"Then here are yer keys!" With a mighty thump, she slapped the keys down on the counter. "Sign here." She whirled the guestbook around, jabbing one spider-like finger at the register.

I signed and took the keys but, for a moment, she held onto them. "May ye sleep peacefully," she said, "*the nicht.*"

"And the same to ye, Mrs. McNaughton." I tugged at the keys, and she let them go. "Will ye show us to our rooms?"

She gave a sharp intake of breath and put a hand to her breast. "There are but twa rooms to the inn, Mr. McCracken," she explained. "I ken the man who has foond his wa' frae London can find his wa' tae his ruim. Thank the Guid Lord ye dinna have to sleep i' the carriage hoose. And a bonnie nicht to the lot of ye."

She slammed the register closed and pierced me with her glare as we all trooped up the stairs and found our rooms.

Ours was a neat little room with whitewashed walls and heavy time-blackened beams overhead. The one small window was framed with scarlet curtains, and on the wall hung another

McNaughton portrait, dour and uncompromising. A couple of oil lamps stood on the heavy oak dresser, and a rocking chair rested in the small bay window.

"What was all that about?" wondered Ari, as Fritz started putting the clothes away. She set Archie down on the floor and, good and faithful son he is, he immediately started exploring. "And why are you whistling?"

"No reason," I replied. Opening the window, I looked out over a lichen-covered slate roof towards the shadowed street below. All was bluing as the night drew on. "My, but it's good to be home!" Archie muttered quietly under his breath that actually it wasn't a home, it was a hotel, but I turned a blind eye to his gaping error.

I looked intently at Ari. "Is something wrong?" There was a crease between her perfectly-sculpted eyebrows, and her deep, chocolate-brown eyes were wide and staring.

"I got about one word in three down there," she told me despairingly. "What on earth were you talking about?"

I hesitated. What had we been talking about? Ari would disapprove of old Highland feuds, I was sure. But I couldn't lie to her. "We were talking about old times."

Ari's lips pursed and her eyes became angry dots. "About your feud?"

Darn the woman, I thought. She could see right through me, always. "That might have been an element in our conversation, aye."

She pressed her lips together in that disapproving way she had, but before she could elaborate on her understanding of the subject, I said, "You learned four different languages this winter, and once you learned a language nobody in the West had ever heard before in a single day. And you don't understand the dialect of your own husband?" My eye alighted on a couple of books sandwiched between a couple of heavy stone bookends on the dresser. One was the King James Bible. I pulled out the other and handed it to Ari. "There. If you're finding it difficult to understand people, just read that."

"I think I read Robert Burns back in college," said Ari slowly.

"Burns and Shakespeare divide the world between them," I said, quoting someone or other. "There is no third." Ari cocked a skeptical eyebrow and opened the little volume. Lowering herself into the rocking chair, she became rapidly involved in it.

I looked out of the window. The sun had set, leaving my homeland in almost total darkness, but for the gentle golden globes of light that hung around the gas-lamps in the street. It was so hard to believe that this was the day that had brought me a death-defying chase along the roof of a moving train. Would the rest of our trip be just as dangerous?

Of course it would be—but we didn't know just how much at that time.

CHAPTER 7
THE GATHERING

The next morning, after breakfast ("It's nae much," said Mrs. McNaughton, "but it's guid honest vittles, and guid enough fer a papist and a *McCracken*"), and since the Gathering at the Castle wasn't due to start until the afternoon, I took Archie for a walk through the streets of "Auld Reekie." In spite of its name, it wasn't very smoky that morning, and the day was bright and clear as we walked down the Royal Mile, saw Greyfriars Kirk and passed by John Knox's house. We made our approach to the castle along a narrow street, where we found an old Catholic church, sandwiched between two grey houses.

"I haven't been to confession in a while," I confided to Archie. "Shall we go in?" Archie's attention was riveted upon a milk cart, drawn by a massive Shire horse with shaggy hoofs, but he was able to pull his eyes away from the spectacle for long enough to give a nod. We entered the church and, genuflecting, sat before the Blessed Sacrament for a few minutes. The smell of the old wood and the incense was strong, mixed with a faint dampness that decades of rain had made indelible. A short line of penitents stood waiting beside the confessional and presently Archie and I joined them.

"Forgive me, Father, for I have sinned," I said, a few minutes later. "It's been—" I thought hard. "—a little over three weeks since my last confession."

There was a long pause, then: "May the Lord help you to know and confess your sins."

"Feshoo shins," commented Archie.

Another longish pause. "My son, is there a bairn in the confessional with you?" asked the priest.

"There is, Father."

"You great heathen!" thundered the voice through the screen. "Do you want your bairn to be privy to all your heinous sins?"

"He's not yet three, Father."

"God save us, but you're arguing with a priest now. The Sacrament is a private matter between the Good Lord and yourself. Leave the child outside, will you!"

"Sorry, Father."

"Aye, and so you should be."

I took Archie outside, and hesitated for a moment. What could I do with him? I couldn't leave him to roam about inside the church.

"Och, but there's a sweet-faced little bairn you have, sure enough," said an old lady in the confession line.

"Thank you, ma'am," I replied, and looked about for inspiration.

Behind me, the door to the confessional opened and closed. Casting a fearful glance behind me, I caught sight of a heavy-set figure in cassock and purple stole, his silvering beard bristling like the quills of a fretful porcupine. I almost dropped Archie in surprise.

"Father Jamie!" I cried. "What are you doing here?"

"Apart from bringing heathens like you into the light of God's truth," replied my old friend, "I'm here with your Mam and Dad." He stepped in close to me, cocked his head on one side, and glared at me with those eyes that seemed to strip away everything save your soul. "Did you ken they were here, or, faithless soul you are, did you think you could sneak into the Home of the Brave without you tell your own blood?" My eyes dropped towards my feet, and Fr. Jamie held up a hand. He saw something that seemed to cause all his ire to drain away. "Och, but I can see you've been having a sore time of it all. This War will be the marring of many a soul. Only Our Good Lord can sort it all out now. Dinna fash yourself about it, but leave it for confession. I'm here to provide the Sacraments for the faithful half who'll be at the Gathering this afternoon. This feud has been going on far too long!" His eyes lighted upon Archie. "Is this handsome fellow your own, then?"

"He is. Fr. Jamie, meet Archie McCracken. Archie, meet the man who baptized your Dad and saved his life in Portugal, Fr. Jamie Erickson. Say How do you do, Archie."

"How-dee-do," said Archie dutifully; but he hid behind my leg and peeked out at Fr. Jamie.

Fr. Jamie, showing all his teeth in a broad smile, took Archie's pudgy little hand in his own and shook it. "And how do you do yourself, my bonnie wee lad. I'm glad you've got a better grasp of the Fourth Commandment than your Da."

"Fourth Commandment?" I said, mainly to rile Fr. Jamie, "Is that the one about stealing?"

"Och, but I'm among the pagans! But you, young Archie, you're a good loyal Catholic soul, are you not? You got that from your Ma, I reckon. Archibald? That's a brave Scots name, young laddie."

"Except that his name is actually Archimedes—a clever Greek name."

Fr. Jamie's face twisted into a grimace. "Faugh, so you've gone all Greek on me! Have you no sense of decency? This is what comes of all your traipsing around the world—you lose all sense of good taste. But anyhow, I'll hear your confession now, if you'll leave the bairn with one of these good ladies."

About three of the ladies in the confession line stepped forward to volunteer their services, and I went into the confessional with my old friend, leaving Archie in more than capable hands. My confession took only a short time, and after my penance, I left the church with a light heart, knowing I could persuade Fr. Jamie to join us on this new adventure. I was sure we'd all be safe with the brawny priest protecting us body and soul.

As we emerged from the church, I saw a shadowy figure dodge into an alleyway ahead of us. My heart seemed to leap into my throat, but I quickened my pace, reached the alleyway, and stared down it. It was utterly deserted, though I could hear a woman's voice singing through an upper-story window.

It would be good, I thought, as Archie and I made our way back to the inn, that someone else would be coming along to share and hopefully divide all the dangers of the next few days.

* * *

Edinburgh Castle is built on a rocky outcrop that overlooks the Auld Reekie, and is visible from all parts of the town, an indomitable monument to the unconquerable Scottish spirit. As we approached the gates across the Esplanade, where the Tattoo and other military ceremonies occur, the flat report of a 32-pound gun sounded off to our right. I flinched at the noise, and Ari, resplendent in a flowing dark-blue dress with red piping, shot a glance at me.

"It's just the one o'clock gun," I reassured her. "They've been setting it off for years now."

"Why?"

I shrugged. "A time signal for ships in the harbour down below." We walked on a moment. "It reminded me of the artillery in France too. I don't know why I would flinch. I've heard guns before."

Ari squeezed my hand for reassurance, and we walked on.

At the far end of the Esplanade, a gateway was planted in the middle of high walls that reached out like a pair of arms. On either side of the gate were sentry boxes, outside of which stood kilted Black Watch privates with tall busbies and rifles. We passed between them and along a narrow passage that turned a few times till we found ourselves in a courtyard, surrounded by stone buildings three and four stories high, one with a turret. Ahead of us was our destination, and we joined the throng entering the Great Hall.

Inside, the Great Hall was spacious, paneled to about head-height, and painted scarlet above that. Suits of armour stood against the walls, and over a wide fireplace, spears and claymores were displayed in great shining fan-shapes. The Great Hall was filled with people, the men almost all kilted, the women in a variety of colours and styles, but most with a flash of tartan somewhere about them.

"Cracky!" boomed a voice, and up swept Fr. Jamie, pumped my hand, and raised Ari's fingers to kiss them.

"Fr. Jamie!" exclaimed Ari with a broad smile. "How wonderful to see you again!"

Fr. Jamie's eyes hardened as he looked at me. "And I think you know these people, Cracky," he said coolly.

"Mum! Dad!" I exclaimed, as Fr. Jamie stepped aside to reveal a man with unkempt white hair in a crumpled argyle jacket and the somewhat more elegant form of my mother. A moment later I found myself wrapped in their embraces. My mother wiped away a little tear.

"Welcome hame tae ye!" cried my Dad. "Ah see ye've git yersel' a bonnie wee lass tae gudwife! Och, mon, but she's a bonnie hen!"

"Haud yer wheesht, Dad," chided my mother. "Well, Cogs, ye're lookin' guid, Ah cannae ken mah bairn's soo grand a chiel noo!"

"Och, Mam, dinnae make a soch!" I replied. "Dad, fit loch en? Hoo's wark?"

"'Tis a wee bit whiest, Cogs. Ah hae written tae the government, but they wilne write back. Ah thocht if they kenned ye wus mah bairn, they micht hae responded, but nae, nae, 'twas nae soo."

"Hoo'd it wark wi' them metal teeth fer closin' yer trews?" I asked.

"Some Yankee be the name o' Sundbank nicked the patent richt oot from under mah nose," answered my father, somewhat irritably.

"An' this mun be mah new dochter," smiled my Mum, turning to Ari.

Ari smiled at them, back and forth, for a few seconds. Realizing she had been addressed, she blinked, swallowed, and looked at me for help.

"Are ye a'richt, waif?" I asked.

"What are you all saying?" she asked.

"Cannae ye tell that, waif?" I responded. "And ye sae canny wi' the tongues, an' all. We're jist passin' the teem a' dee."

"Wha's this?" said my father in surprise. "Ye married feeve year, an' ye've no learned yer waif yer ane tung?" He shook his head sadly, clicking his tongue in disapproval. "Well, Ah'm sair grieved ye went tae America fer a waif, laddie," he added. "'Twas in mah heid ye micht find yersel' a highland wench to settle doon wi'. But this is a bonnie lass a'richt. Well doon, lad, well doon."[1]

---

[1] For those who, like myself at the time, are unfamiliar with the Scots dialect, the following is a more-or-less accurate translation of the exchange between my husband and his parents on this occasion:

MR. MCCRACKEN: Welcome home to you. I see you have married well! I believe she appears to be a fine, intelligent and capable woman.

MRS. MCCRACKEN: Speak with some reservation, Husband. Well, Cogs [a childhood nickname of my husband's], you appear to be doing well. I find it hard to believe my child has grown up so!

MAC: Oh, Mother, do not make such a fuss. Father, how are you? How is your work?

MR. MCCRACKEN: It is a little difficult, Cogs. I have written to the government, but they have not replied. I thought if they knew you were my son, they might have been more willing to respond, but no, it was not to be.

MAC: How was your work with those metal teeth for fastening one's pants?

MR. MCCRACKEN: An American named Sundbank entered the patent before I was able to do it myself.

MRS. MCCRACKEN: This, no doubt, is my new daughter-in-law.

MAC: Are you well, beloved wife?

ARIADNE: I am experiencing some difficulty following the conversation, owing to the speed of

Some applause began at the far end of the hall, the end where the high table had been set up in front of the fireplace. The applause spread like fire through a dry forest, and we all found ourselves clapping for we knew not what. Then a man appeared behind the table and held up a hand in greeting. From his slicked grey hair and heavy, fleshy features, I knew him at once.

"Sir Timothy LaGrange," I said.

"Ah, so that's who it is, then?" said Fr. Jamie under his breath.

The crowd moved in towards Sir Timothy, who was apparently reorganizing a sheaf of papers. Fr. Kerr hovered in the shadows behind him. After a few moments, Sir Timothy cleared his throat and began speaking. I could hear his

---

delivery and large proportion of lexical items and syntactic structures of a dialectal nature.

MAC: I am greatly surprised you cannot follow our conversation. I know well and highly esteem your reputation for languages; the fault is no doubt mine. We are merely greeting one another and catching up on family news.

MR. MCCRACKEN: My son, how can it be in five years of married life you have so neglected your wife as to never introduce her to our dialect? Well, I believe that marrying an American, and one so accomplished at that, was a very good choice indeed. My congratulations to you. [Translation: Ariadne Bell McCracken]

voice, but I couldn't distinguish words at this distance, so glancing at Ari, I moved forward with the others.

". . . sort of frank conversation I really enjoy. And we can all enjoy that conversation now: McNaughton, McCracken, once the War is over, these distinctions will cease to mean anything. Then, we will all be united as citizens of Scotland."

"Home rule for Scotland!" called out someone near the front of the crowd, and there came a rumble of agreement from McNaughtons *and* McCrackens. Some of them beat their wine-glasses against the table-tops.

Sir Timothy held up his hands, palms outward. "I see there's an issue here that will unite even the clans McNaughton and McCracken! But let's not go back to the Dark Ages, ladies and gentlemen. Tribalism is the way of the past; united, together, we can march into the future! These have been years of great change, ladies and gentlemen—who, a hundred years ago, could have foreseen the motor-car, the steam-ship, the telephone? It's time now to throw away the old and bring in the new. It's time to put out the horse to pasture and crank up the automobile. And we have to work—work for the future, work for our great nation!" More applause. Sir Timothy waited for it to die down, then went on: "It's machines, ladies and gentlemen of the McNaughton and McCracken clans, machines that will lead us into this bright future. I see a future in which food is canned by machines, children taught by machines, people flown on vacation by the sea in machines. And the machine begins today." A smattering of applause. "We can build those machines now—McNaughtons and McCrackens working side by side to create a shiny new tomorrow, the mechanized future that means wealth and peace and leisure for all!"

There was a fair amount of clapping at this conclusion, but I looked sideways at Ari and Fr. Jamie. "I'm a little suspicious," I said quietly. "I mean, I like machines, but doesn't all that sound a bit . . . cold?"

"He's not a good public speaker," added Ari. "I can't quite figure out what he said."

"I'd like to hear his plan," concluded Fr. Jamie, in a tone of voice that said unequivocally that he didn't expect to like it. "The machine begins today? It's eternal life that begins today."

"Och, but isn't he *wonderful*!" My mother's hands were clasped before her heart.

At that point, Sir Timothy looked up from the crowd that had gathered about him, and our eyes clicked together. For a moment, and perhaps it was just my imagination, it seemed that something like fire flashed behind them. But then, like a roller blind snapping up, that fire was gone and he smiled broadly. It was even a genuine smile, as if he really liked me. He excused himself to the people around him, glanced quickly back at Fr. Kerr, and made his way towards us.

CHAPTER 8
THE CARD SHARP

Before they reached us, Sir Timothy and Fr. Kerr were joined by a distinguished gentleman in waistcoat and Jacobite shirt, with a great kilt of the McNaughton plaid. Sir Timothy and the gentleman spoke together for a few moments, then resumed moving towards us, the gentleman accompanying them.

"Have you met Sir Timothy before, then?" asked Fr. Jamie.

I nodded. "In France."

"I had no idea you'd come up so far in the world, Cracky," murmured Fr. Jamie, as the three of them arrived.

"Mr. McCracken!" Sir Timothy took my hand in a brief, dry clasp. "How very pleasant to meet you again. It hasn't been a fortnight since last we met, but you've been very much in my thoughts since then."

"And you in mine, Sir Timothy," I answered him. My mother looked as if she were going to faint. I did a quick round of introductions.

"Mrs. McCracken," said Sir Timothy, after he had kissed Ari's hand, "your husband and I enjoyed a very frank conversation recently in

France. It was exactly the kind of conversation I enjoy—completely honest and to the point, with no reservations. Isn't that right, Mr. McCracken?" I gave him a tight-lipped smile. "Now, let me introduce you all to someone. This is Sir Alexander McNaughton, the organizer of this event."

"Sir Timothy," flustered Sir Alexander, "you're too modest—this Gathering would never have been possible without your funds!"

"Just doing my bit, Sir Alexander, just doing my bit," answered Sir Timothy.

Sir Alexander beamed as he gazed around him at the throng. "Almost three hundred years, and finally there can be a reconciliation—this is a great day!"

"And how will that reconciliation be achieved, Sir Alexander?" asked Fr. Jamie.

Sir Alexander turned his radiant smile upon him. "Fellowship," he said, "that emerges from food and pleasant pastimes. Tonight we feast, then we play card games. Tomorrow, there will be Highland Games."

"Food and games will bring the enemies together, then?" Sir Alexander nodded.

"Perhaps we should try that with the Germans," I interjected.

There was a little laughter at that suggestion. "If I remember correctly, Mr. McCracken, that was tried, back at the Christmas of '14. We heard rumours of soldiers from Britain, France and Germany playing football and sharing Christmas feasts. The Brass put a stop to that in quick order, I can tell you. War is war. Peace is peace. The McNaughtons and the McCrackens are not such deep enemies as we and the Germans. After all, the McCrackens are not, as the Kaiser is, tyrants!"

More polite laughter followed this remark, though Ari's smile seemed strained to me.

"So, Mr. McCracken," said Sir Timothy, turning to me, "this is our second meeting. Now, my friends in Chicago have a saying. Have you ever been to Chicago?" Ari opened her mouth to reply, for she had graduated from the University of Chicago, but Sir Timothy did not seem to have noticed her. "They say, 'The first meeting is happenstance, the second coincidence, but the third is enemy action.' Our first meeting was happenstance, indeed, nothing more. That means this meeting is a coincidence—I'm willing to believe that. Our third ought to be enemy action, but I know I've invited you to visit my plant on Frith. So perhaps my friends in Chicago are wrong. What do you think, Mr. McCracken?"

"Perhaps by 'enemy action' they mean . . ." I began, but Sir Timothy interrupted me with a firm hand on my shoulder.

"Of course, of course! Not enemy action, but certainly a deliberate choice. I should have known you'd see that, Mr. McCracken." Sir Timothy's eyes narrowed. "What an incisive mind you have! I wouldn't have thought of that, but you went right to it. See, Mrs. McCracken? This is exactly what I was talking about. This is the kind of honest conversation your husband and I enjoyed before, in France."

"Is the invitation still open, Sir Timothy?" I asked.

Sir Timothy gave a short laugh. "Of course it is, Mr. McCracken, of course it is! You know, Mrs. McCracken, I really enjoy your husband's company—we struck it off right away. I always like an honest man to talk to, and your husband tells it like it is. But for sure there's still an invitation for you, Mr. McCracken. Bring Mrs. McCracken with you too—I think she'll be very interested in the school we're operating there."

"School?"

"Yes, school. Education is one of the things we do. Hasn't your husband told you? But none of that silly stuff, not poems and rubbish. Science. Business. Technology. Our graduates will be useful citizens! We're expecting a visit from the President of the Board of Education within the next few days—do you know Herbert Fisher? If he has his way, school will soon be compulsory until the age of fourteen in this country, and everyone will get the same education, whether they're in Edinburgh or Birmingham or Cardiff."

"Imagine that," commented Ari drily.

"Yes, *think* how useful that will be! And we're starting the experiment at Frith Academy."

"And there's the canned food too, right, Sir Timothy?"

"Yes, yes, the canned food. You'll be eating some of it tonight. Not the salad—I haven't found a way of canning that yet. But certainly the cullen skink and the haggis. Well, it's been nice talking to you. I do enjoy honest discussions! Nice to meet you, Mrs. McCracken."

With a nod to Fr. Jamie and my parents, he was off, leaving us wondering what on earth we had discussed at all.

The afternoon went on very pleasantly, and I met a number of my relatives that I hadn't seen in years, almost in decades. Waiters circulated among us, bearing silver trays on which rested glasses of whisky, and I took one for myself and one for my Dad, and we busied ourselves in a discussion about the inventions he'd been trying to patent, how business was in his ironmonger shop, and my travels to different parts of the world over the last few years. When the food came, it was actually quite good, and I ate perhaps a little more than I should have, though I missed Fritz's deft hand and subtle nose in the kitchen. Cullen skink is a type of fish soup with onion and mashed potatoes, delightfully smoky in its flavour. With it came haggis, or minced lamb and onions, seasoned with lots of salt and pepper and soaked in gravy. Finally came dessert: raspberry buns with shortbread, which occasioned a brief argument between me and Ari, since she insisted on calling them *cookies*, when they're clearly *biscuits*.

Finally, the food was cleared away, and out came the cards. Groups broke up into rubbers of bridge, games of whist, or pontoon, that Americans call blackjack. The canasta players slung their jackets over the backs of their seats and rolled up their sleeves. They were preparing for a long conflict, like a war.

A small band consisting of a couple of fiddlers, a piper and a drummer struck up the first of a series of stirring tunes. A space was cleared near the band, and tentatively at first, couples began to dance the reel. Before long, they were joined by others, until the dance floor was full.

"Games, dancin' and *aqua vitae*." Grinning, I raised my glass of whisky to Ari. "Ah, Scotland the Brave!"

We danced a little, chatted often to members of my distant family, ate little snacks, drank a little whisky, and the evening wore on. I enjoy playing card games, but it's not always what I want to do. The air about the tables was thick with cigarette-smoke, and I was reminded of the smoke that hung over no-man's land. In any case, I've never enjoyed tobacco, and found it slightly nauseating. Ari and I spoke to various people who were there, with caution to a number of McNaughtons.

A couple of hours after the games had begun, Ari and I were beginning to think of returning to the inn when my father wandered up. He looked confused.

"Are you all right, Dad?" I asked.

My father shook his head slowly. "It's that LaGrange," he said. "I dinna ken how he's doing it."

"Doing what, Dad?"

Dad made a gesture back at the card tables. "He's brought a new-fangled game wi' him from America. He calls it *poker* or some such nonsense. I didnae play, but I warked oot the rules after a few hands. And I'm sure of this, though I cannae figure oot hoo he does it—he's cheatin'."

"Cheating!" I exclaimed in surprise.

"Who's cheating?" asked Ari, so I explained quickly what my father had said. "How does this *poker* game work?" I asked.

"It's very mathematical," replied Ari. "You're dealt five cards. You can replace a certain number of them with fresh cards to try and beat your opponents; some five-card combinations are ranked higher than others. You pay an *ante*, which is a sum of money to play; then you bet on the likelihood of your beating the other players. When everyone has placed his bet, you reveal your cards, and the winner takes all the money that's been placed."

"How do you calculate the odds of winning?"

Ari smiled. "That's where the fun is. You can figure out how strong a player's hand is by how he acts—how he gambles, how he reacts on seeing his cards, that kind of thing. You can also bluff—gamble in such a way that you imply your hand is stronger than it is. In that way, you can trick them into giving up."

"So the whole game is based of cheating?"

"No. No one lies, no one cheats—you let other players draw their own conclusions. This is a very popular game back in America right now, especially on the frontier, or what used to be the frontier about forty years ago."

"Is there any pattern to LaGrange's winning, Dad?"

"A bit." My Dad thought about it for a moment. "When he's the dealer, he wins a lot. If someone else is banker, he plays a very cautious game. He sometimes loses the hand, but he doesn't lose much money. Of course, he's playing with folks that don't know the game so well as he does."

"If there aren't any limits on the gambling," Ari put in, "then LaGrange can throw his money around to dominate the jackpot."

"He's a bully," I said. "That's the kind of thing he'd do. I doubt if I can figure it out, but I'll see if I can catch anything."

We made our way over to the poker table, which had drawn a large crowd. Smoke wound up from the cigarettes of several players, but LaGrange did not smoke, though a bright silver cigarette case lay on the felt before him.

The hand had just begun, and there was a pile of coins in the centre of the table. LaGrange matched the bets coming from the other players and, when someone else raised, he followed. One player tapped on the table and slid two cards towards the dealer. The dealer gave him two cards back. The next asked for one, and so on. LaGrange asked for two cards. There was nothing to be seen yet. Faint beads of sweat shone on the dome of a McCracken forehead. A McNaughton tapped his finger lightly on the table-top and then raised the bet. A couple of players folded, but LaGrange stayed in and increased the bet. The McNaughton matched him. LaGrange raised again. A faint half-smile played over his lips.

"I don't think he's cheating." The crowd was dense around us, and I had to whisper. "He's just playing this McNaughton really well."

"I wouldn't have thought he paid enough attention to other people to play this game well," Ari observed. "That trait of his is a perfect smokescreen."

Smokescreen. Something moved sluggishly in my mind, but I had to focus on the game. There were just two players left: the McNaughton and LaGrange. LaGrange's turn came and, after a long consideration of his cards, he pushed a massive pile of coins into the centre of the table. "Call," he said.

The McNaughton shook his head. "That's too much for me, LaGrange," he said, sliding his cards towards the dealer face-down. "It's a canny way you have of knowing those cards. I've seen nothing like it."

"He didn't know the cards," Ari whispered to me. "He just used his money to bully him out of the game."

"The deal's passing to him," I replied.

LaGrange took the pack, shuffled them and cut them. I watched carefully. Each card wobbled in flight as he dealt them, and the slight movement . . .

No! I thought. Not possible.

LaGrange won this hand, quite a large jackpot. He played a cautious hand next, and lost, but only a small amount. The same with the next hand. I just needed to see him deal again to confirm my suspicions. In the end, play passed to LaGrange. He shuffled and dealt, and now I was sure.

"I think I know what's going on. Let's have a little fun with Mr. LaGrange," I whispered to Ari, and slipped away from her, making my way through the crowd towards LaGrange.

CHAPTER 9
HIGHLAND GAMES

It took me a little while to get through the crowd so that I stood behind Sir Timothy, and even then I didn't watch the game for the time being. I was preparing for what I had to do next. I had to wait until LaGrange next dealt.

The pack came to him, and he was shuffling.

"It's quite a winning streak you're having, LaGrange," I commented.

He gave a little jump, as if he had not noticed me before. Flashing white teeth up at me, he commented, "I don't like to lose, Mr. McCracken."

"That's a beautiful cigarette case," I said, leaning forward to pick it up and examine it.

Perhaps it was my imagination, but it seemed to me that for a brief moment an expression of uncertainty flitted across LaGrange's brow and eyes, gone in an instant and perhaps never there. After all, my angle was a poor one.

"Hurry up, LaGrange," said one of the players. "Don't ye think you've shuffled enough?"

"I'll get to it, Mr. McNaughton," answered LaGrange. I snapped open the cigarette case, selected a cigarette, and put it between my lips. With some obvious reluctance, LaGrange began dealing. Striking a match, I lit the cigarette and drew the smoke into my lungs.

It was horrible. Foul-tasting, burning, I couldn't understand why it was such a popular pastime. My head had begun to swim, but I had to appear totally unconcerned. Across the table, Ari watched me, her eyes wide in amazement. She started moving off through the crowd.

LaGrange had finished with his deal, and I replaced the cigarette case beside his elbow. Blowing out a cloud of smoke I whispered, so quietly only he could hear, "I know your game, LaGrange. I think your luck ought to change. I don't think Sir Alexander would be very impressed with what you're doing."

LaGrange's eyes flicked up at mine. He peered under the corners of his own cards, then across at the nervous players. He rapped gently on the table with his knuckles.

"Oh, I think you ought to *lose* a little money, don't you?" I said, and stayed until he had bid a sizeable pile.

I wandered away from the table, stubbing out the cigarette with about two inches more left. Behind me, a great cheer went up from the poker table.

"Mac, are you okay?" It was Ari, her eyes deeply troubled, with my father just behind her.

"No, that was the most horrible thing I've ever put into my mouth," I commented, taking a glass of whisky from a passing waiter and slamming it.

"I've never seen you smoke before," Ari went on, "except cigars. What made you do that?"

"Did you find out how he was doin' it, son?" asked my father.

I nodded. "Most of the time, he just used his money to bully people out of the game," I explained. "But on his deal, he would pass all the cards over that shiny cigarette case. It was like a mirror. He could see the faces of all the cards he dealt, and he knew the hand of every player."

"So he *was* cheating!" gasped Ari. Her nose wrinkled in disgust. "Why would he do that? He's got plenty of money!"

"It's not about the money," I explained. "It never is with LaGrange. It's about the power. He likes money because it commands the loyalty of those around him. That's what he likes—being adored and admired."

My father nodded. "And the man who'll cheat at cards will do a lot worse than that."

"That's what I'm afraid of, Dad." Another cheer of victory went up from the poker table, and I saw that one of my own relatives was raking in the pot. Was that it? I wondered. Was it just cheating at cards? Or was there something more sinister at work?

The Highland Games were held the following afternoon on a wide, flat expanse of lush grass fringed by trees on three sides and by stone cottages on the other, five or six miles outside of Edinburgh's city limits. To the skirl of bagpipes and the rousing rattle of the drums, we spread out a blanket on the ground and broke out the picnic lunch Fritz had prepared. God bless him, Fritz had learned to make bannock cakes, which tasted more Scottish than anything my Mum had made when I was a nipper, and shortbread that dissolved instantly in my mouth leaving behind the hint of melted butter that made those biscuits (or *cookies*) so delicious. We watched the caber toss and the hammer throw, and the sword dance. I was roped in—literally—to help with the tug-of-war, which we won because I insisted on putting Fr. Jamie on our team as our anchor.

From time to time during the day, I caught sight of LaGrange, usually with a knot of older, wealthy-looking people from both clans. Fr. Kerr was generally with him, but silent and withdrawn.

"God forgive me speaking ill of a fellow clergyman," remarked Fr. Jamie, "but I do not like that fellow overly well."

"Is his faith unorthodox?" asked Ari.

Fr. Jamie shook his head. "No. But it's too perfect. He had all the right answers, but there wasn't any life in them. It was as if a machine were answering me."

At the end of the day, as we packed up the remnants of our feast and headed towards the omnibus that had brought us from the city, a McNaughton thumped me on the back and pumped my hand, saying, "Well, I still think you McCrackens are a bunch of doaty barmpots, but I'll nae slit yer throats in yer sleep, ye ken!" And it certainly seemed that progress had been made.

As we waited to board the omnibus, LaGrange thrust himself into our group with a wide smile. "Well, that's twice we've met, Mr. McCracken," he enthused, "and I have to say how thoroughly I've enjoyed each occasion." He gave me almost what looked like a wink. "Some would harbour a grudge about what you suggested about me yesterday evening, but I like it—I like your honesty and your frankness. Well done, McCracken, well done! It promises well for our third encounter, wouldn't you say?" I nodded, and was about to say something, but he carried on like a freight train over a bag of bananas: "I'm sure our next meeting will be the most interesting of all, Mr. McCracken. I'm certain of it. In fact, you can count on its being a meeting that will change your life. Absolutely change your life. I think you'll find what we do up on Frith very interesting, very interesting indeed. Well, it's been a pleasure. See you soon, McCracken, Mrs. McCracken."

And he passed on; Fr. Kerr nodded a silent greeting to us and slid after him like his shadow.

Our journey began again the following morning, when we caught a train to Aberdeen, where I had grown up. From there, we were to board a ferry that would take us to the Shetlands. Rain drizzled from a slate-grey sky as we emerged onto the wharf where the *Flora MacDonald*, a paddle steamer with a single tall funnel just forward of the paddles, was moored.

"Look, Archie." I pointed the vessel out to him. "It's a ferry."

"Actually, Daddy, it's a boat." Archie was utterly deadpan.

"No, you see," I argued, "a ferry *is* a boat, a type of boat."

Archie's eyebrows twisted into a skeptical shape. "Actually, Daddy," he insisted with a little more volume, "it's a *boat*."

Fr. Jamie reached out and tousled his hair. "That's it, Sproggin," he said, "don't let that Dad of yours get away with anything."

"Actually," replied the Sproggin, "I'm a boy."

Fr. Jamie guffawed, and we all trooped up the swaying gangplank. Owing to Ari's condition and Fr. Jamie's collar, we were able to get seats around a table, but we were constantly jostled by elbows and shoulders as the twelve-hour trip began. Fr. Jamie bought beers and sandwiches from the bar and a glass of milk for Archie, clapping his change on the table with a metallic clatter. Archie sipped his milk, but looked at our beers with envious eyes.

"Now, Father," said Ari, setting her beer down before her, "you were in Portugal last year. We got your telegram, but what with one thing and another, we couldn't get there. What was happening? You wrote, 'Come soon. Miraculous.'"

Fr. Jamie drank deeply from his mug. "Aye, that it was—a miracle and no doubt." His eyes moved from one to another of us. "You ken, all my life I've searched for the Land of Prester John. When we found that, four years ago, what was there for me to do? More to the point, what did the Good Lord have in mind for me? But this, what I saw in Portugal, this tops it all." We all waited patiently. "It was Our Lady, so it was. Our Lady standing there in all her pure glory."

Ari caught her breath. I said, "Are you serious?"

Fr. Jamie nodded. "As serious as I've ever been. I tell you, it was the Mother of God herself!"

"Did she say anything?" asked Ari.

"Aye," replied Fr. Jamie, "but not to me. She spoke to three wee bairns. Like you, Master Archie." Fr. Jamie fixed Archie with his eye, and Archie looked up at him with trepidation, for the priest had caught him in the act of filching some of his change from the table. Archie raised his hand and offered Fr. Jamie one of his own pennies.

"Money to taste?" he asked.

"Och, and how can you refuse the wee bairn? Here you go, laddie." Fr. Jamie treated Archie to a sip of beer, after which Archie smacked his lips and grinned broadly.

"There's going to come a time," mused Ari, "when that won't be allowed any more. Back in America, there are temperance marchers who want to ban all strong drink by law."

"It hasn't happened yet," I pointed out. "And how could they do that? Whether or not you have a beer or a glass of whisky—that's not the government's business. It's private."

"I think in Germany," said Fritz, "there will be people who will their freedoms surrender if it means that no more will there be war."

"Surrendering your freedom to a government sounds to me like the best way of causing another war," Ari said.

Fr. Jamie thrust out his forefinger triumphantly. "That's exactly it!" he cried. "That's what I was trying to say. That's what Our Lady told these wee bairns. She said that this War would soon be over."

"But that's wonderful!" cried Ari. "It's been going on far too long as it is."

"Aye, but wheesht a moment, my dear," cautioned Fr. Jamie. "She said this War would soon be over but there would be another one, still more terrible, to come."

"How is that even possible?" Ari looked bewildered. "The world has never seen a war more terrible than this one."

"It could happen," I said flatly. "Think of how machines like tanks and aeroplanes have made this war as horrible as it is. Imagine machines that are bigger, more destructive, more accurate." I twisted my lip. "That's Sir Timothy's dream," I concluded, "his shiny new tomorrow."

"Is there anything we can do to avoid it?" Ari asked Fr. Jamie.

Fr. Jamie took a long draught from his beer and nodded slowly. "Our Lady was apparently quite specific about that. She said—and this is going to sound strange—but she said that we must stop Russia from spreading its errors. And then—can you believe it?—she made the sun dance in the sky!"

"She made what?"

"The sun dance in the sky—I saw it with these eyes! It wouldn't stand still. It was spinning, and growing large, and moving from one side to the other. It filled me to the top with awe and wonder, I can tell you."

Ari and I exchanged glances. Fritz's eyes shone.

I cleared my throat. "Fr. Jamie, we saw that too. When did it happen?"

"October last year."

"What date?"

"The 13th—all the visions happened on the 13th day of the month."

Ari closed her eyes a second. "That would work out, given that the Russians use a different calendar from us." She leaned forward across the table. "Fr. Jamie, we saw that. We were in Russia, in Siberia, and saw that miracle."

I've already written the story that describes what happened, so I don't need to do that here. But when Ari had finished relating it to Fr. Jamie, he leaned back in his seat and gave a long, low whistle. "Well now, that's cannie. So you saw that miracle at the same time? But in Russia? Yet there were folks who couldn't see it who were less than a mile away from Fatima."

"We ran into someone the next day who lived close by, and saw nothing," I confirmed.

"Well, isn't that food for the mind!" Fr. Jamie drew in a deep breath. "And for the soul."

"And I think," I said slowly, "I know what she meant by *Russia's errors*."

"That was the strange thing—Russia's hardly a significant world power. What does it matter that she makes errors? I can't think Our Lady meant the Eastern Orthodox Church."

I shook my head. "Communism," I told him.

He nodded slowly. "So, that's the nature of their revolution, is it? But it can hardly spread any further. And who would pay any attention to such a thick-headed idea?"

"There are more thick-headed people around than you ken, Father," I told him.

"Aye, I suppose you're right. The world's a crazy place—communist or fascist, we're creating a world in which wars will start because some poor fool blew his nose in the wrong direction."

The *Flora MacDonald* pitched as she rode a deep trough and then a particularly high wave. Foam splashed the window by which we sat. We each reached out to steady our drinks. Cries of alarm rose from the other passengers. Archie said, "*Whee!*" When the ferry had settled down a bit, Fr. Jamie leaned forward and said confidentially, "Don't make any sudden movements, Cracky, but is there a chance someone might be following you?"

It was difficult not to look over my shoulder, but I managed it, and told Fr. Jamie about the man at King's Cross, the incident on the Scotsman, and the figure I'd seen in Edinburgh.

"So someone's been following you." Fr. Jamie finished off his pint. "There's danger is this adventure, all right," he said. "We should stay together as much as we can."

And the *Flora MacDonald* ploughed on through the choppy seas towards our date with danger.

CHAPTER 10
THE CASTLE

We nosed between two headlands and moored at the quay of Lerwick, a grey-stoned and slate-roofed town between treeless hills, in the early evening. The smell of fish and seawater billowed from the wharf, mingling with the steel and oil of the ferry, as we trooped down the gangplank and into the town. Ari pointed to the ranks of fishing vessels alongside us. "Most of those flags are Norwegian," she observed.

"We're almost as close to Norway here as to Scotland," I explained. "Actually, the Shetland Isles used to belong to Norway. Every new year, they pull a great big Viking longship through the town here and burn it on the beach while everyone has a party."

"Sounds delightful," commented Ari.

Among the fishermen in thick sweaters and peaked caps moved a fair number of men in khaki uniforms and kilts. "I wonder who they are?" I asked Fr. Jamie.

"They're the Gordon Highlanders," came a voice. Turning, we found ourselves faced by a young man, probably in his late twenties, with a mop of sandy hair, wearing a tweed jacket and a faded red tie. "They've been recruited from the Islands, and ship out to France next week." He thrust out a hand, which we all shook in turn. "I'm Charlie McGross, one of the masters at Frithoway Academy. I'm supposed to take you on the last leg of your voyage to the Isle of Frith. I say, young man." He went down on his haunches to talk to Archie. "You must be a brave sailor—the sea's been pretty choppy today. It's a commodore you'll be before you're very much older. Is this your car?" He pointed to the toy Archie had been playing with on the voyage.

Archie held up the toy car. "Actually, it's a Studebaker."

"I see. Can you tell me what the parts are?"

Archie pointed here and there on the toy. "That the wheel, that the door, that the carburetor."

"Carburetor?" said McGross in disbelief.

"Under the hood," explained Archie.

"The hood?" McGross raised an eyebrow. "You mean the bonnet?"

"Actually, that's not a bonnet, it's a hood."

"I'm afraid he's learned some of his terms from me," Ari explained with a laugh. "It comes with Mac being out of the house so much. You seem to make friends very easily, Mr. McGross."

McGross gave a lop-sided grin. "Most especially with the young 'uns. Sometimes, I feel like the Pied Piper." Ruffling Archie's hair, he straightened and spoke to the grown-ups. "I have a motor-launch moored just along the wharf. I'm one of the few masters who can handle it, so naturally Miss Major sent me to fetch you."

"Miss Major?"

"The headmistress. You'll meet her soon. The launch is this way. Would you follow me, please?"

He led us to a twenty-foot motor-launch with a small cabin housing the helm and an Evinrude outboard motor in the stern. Wooden seats in the stern were sheltered by a canvas roof overhead.

"Would you like to help me steer, Captain Archie?" asked McGross, and Archie climbed down from Ari's lap and toddled forward with enthusiasm to join him in the wheelhouse.

We were underway shortly after. This stage of the journey was relatively brief, and before long a small island reared up out of the waves before us. From the wheelhouse, McGross pointed at an outcrop of rock projecting from the cliffs, and falling vertiginously and directly into foaming waters below.

"Laird's Leap!" he explained. "It's a legend in these parts, about Laird Alastair, sometime during the Killing Times—what you'd call the

English Civil War. Laird Alastair had but one son, and him a traitor to the Scottish Kirk. He'd determined to marry a pretty golden-haired English girl, you see. Well, Lord Alastair had his revenge. Turning up to the wedding celebration, he ran his sword up to the hilts through his own son, then rode and rowed all the way from Carlisle back to this forlorn island. And it's from that rock he leaped, and that was the end of his line entirely."

Ari and I gulped. Ari went forward and picked Archie up.

The boat rounded the headland, and there before us we could see the slate roof of an old stone building, rising above the surrounding houses at the wharf.

"That's Frithoway Academy," yelled McGross to us.

It was a typical tower house, I saw as we neared it, with bartizans at each of the four corners. A chimney pierced the roof at the north end, and from that rose a lazy trail of smoke. The windows seemed to have been placed randomly in the wall facing us, with the result that it was difficult to tell whether there were four stories or only three. Another couple of young men, these wearing academic regalia, met us at the wharf, and while McGross tied the launch up, they took our luggage.

The sun was setting behind thick grey clouds as we followed the teachers between the little houses, the wind cool on our backs, towards the castle. A wrought iron fence of relatively modern manufacture surrounded the whole fortress and its grounds, and a gravel driveway led from the tall gates to the door, which was reached by a short flight of steps. As with most medieval fortifications, there were no windows on the ground floor, for purposes of defence. As we approached, the door opened and we filed inside.

"I'll see you later, Archie," said McGross, tickling Archie and ruffling his hair. Then he led the others, with our luggage, up a wide flight of stairs.

We found ourselves in a wide hallway with stairs running to a landing above our heads. Doors led off left and right, and ahead of us, through some more modern glass doors, we could see some tall hedges, bluing now in the dusk. The walls were covered with claymores and bucklers, portraits of long-dead lairds, and huge many-branched candelabra. Suits of armour stood at attention on either side of a flight of stairs, and there were also stuffed game, a deer in one corner and a black bear, bagged most likely in America, in another.

"Mr. McCracken, I presume?"

A female voice had hailed us, and I turned to face a woman of about sixty with short hair, hollow cheeks, and clothes that seemed to be all vertical lines. With a smile that showed no teeth, she offered her hand. "I am Miss Major, Headmistress of the Frithoway Academy."

"I'm McCracken," I said, shaking her hand. "Edinburgh?"

The smile held for a moment longer. "Very perceptive of you, Mr. McCracken. Ingliston. And this would be your lovely wife, of course."

"Ariadne McCracken," said Ari, shaking hands. "Pleasure to meet you."

Miss Major cocked an eyebrow. "Manhattan?" she guessed. "But I think there's a trace of something else there. Were you raised close to the Mexican border, Mrs. McCracken?"

Ari nodded. "My folks have a ranch in New Mexico," she explained.

I introduced Miss Major to everyone else, after which she said, "I'm afraid Sir Timothy is not yet back from the Gathering—you seem to have beaten him, Mr. McCracken. But he'll see you tomorrow after breakfast. I'm afraid I must be your hostess for the moment. Would you care for a glass of something, or would you prefer to bathe first?"

"I'd love a glass of Scotch," I admitted.

"Oh goodness no, Mr. McCracken," answered Miss Major. "We do not serve alcohol at Frithoway Academy. I was referring to water, milk, or perhaps a tomato juice."

"Water, thanks." I exchanged a glance with Fr. Jamie.

"Oh, and if it's not inconvenient, there's to be no smoking while you're at Frithoway, if you please. Sir Timothy's orders."

"Is Sir Timothy a teetotaler?" asked Fr. Jamie.

"No," answered Miss Major, "but it's a bad example for the boys and girls of the Academy."

She led us past the stuffed bear, then up some stairs. On the wall were a stuffed badger and wild cat, then wall mounts of red deer, both does and wide-antlered stags. Eventually, we entered a long room with whitewashed walls and a coffered ceiling. Suits of armour stood in the corners, like silent and rather grim sentinels, and at each end of the room was a tall window giving a view of the harbour and of the castle grounds below.

"Is that a maze, Miss Major?" I asked, pointing through one of the windows.

"It is indeed, Mr. McCracken." Miss Major was pouring beverages. "It is a fascination of Sir Timothy's. At the centre of it is Sir Timothy's canning plant, but I shall let him show you that himself." Again, the prim smile. "That's his hobby."

Ari looked through the window. "In the States, we'd build that out of corn bails. What is that one made from, Miss Major?"

"Privet hedges, Mrs. McCracken."

"How old is this wonderful structure, Miss Major?" asked Fr. Jamie.

"Robert Frith, the Third Laird of Frith, built it in 1599," Miss Major said, slipping into teaching mode. "He had been granted lands by King James, for what services no one is quite sure, and established himself on this island as a powerful but unscrupulous figure. There were complaints against him for misuse of taxes, as well as—ahem—various other misdemeanours. There is said to be the ghost of one of his victims who haunts the lower regions of the castle, particularly around the time of the Hogmanay."

"Oh, that's awful," observed Ari. "Was he related to Laird Alastair?"

"Robert was Alastair's father, and the stories say Alastair was—how would you put it, Mrs. McCracken?—a chip off the old block."

"Awful, as you say, Ariadne," said Fr. Jamie, "like most history. But we ignore it at our own risk."

Miss Major gave her smile. "Who was it who said, 'History always repeats itself, first as a tragedy, second as a farce?'"

"I believe that was Karl Marx, Miss Major," said Fr. Jamie mildly.

"Oh dear me," said Miss Major primly, "I seem to have got my quotation from a disreputable source."

"Truth is still truth, wherever it comes from," Fr. Jamie observed with a broad gesture of the hand that held his glass of water. "What makes it disreputable is the warping of truth for a base purpose."

"Why, whatever can you mean by that, Fr. Erikson?" Miss Major set down her glass of tomato juice.

"Well, take Marx as your example. His facts are correct, but he assembles them in such a way as to imply an evil. It's very true that the working classes in England were kept in very poor conditions as recently as sixty years ago. He uses that to justify violence and the forcible removing of freedoms from God's people."

Miss Major stared at Fr. Jamie for a few moments with blank eyes. They were very blue. When it seemed that no one would ever say anything again, she finally spoke. "Well, that's a very interesting point of view, Fr. Erikson. Thank goodness you and I are from the land of the free, eh?" Catching me out of the corner of her eye, she added, "And you too, of course, Mr. McCracken."

"Miss Major." Ari set down her glass and pried his glass out of Archie's fingers—he had fallen asleep on her lap. "Can you tell us about what you do here at Frithoway?"

"I certainly can, Mrs. McCracken. "As you know, education has recently been made accessible to people of all social classes. What Sir Timothy has realized is that there is therefore a great need for what you might call a common core of knowledge that we can guarantee will be taught to all students in British schools, delivered by a single teaching method, the method most efficient in delivering such information."

"Can you give me an example?" asked Ari.

"Well, we need to be able to guarantee that students all over the United Kingdom know exactly the same material. It's a question of cultural literacy. A student in Edinburgh, in Glasgow, in Birmingham or Exeter or Cardiff will learn the multiplication tables at exactly the same point in their academic careers. They will all learn the same geography, the same chemistry, the same foreign language and at the same time. Everyone will know exactly what everyone else knows."

"I see. The same mathematics, the same poetry, the same art."

"Ah yes," replied Miss Major. "Of course, poetry for the lower forms. It is an excellent way to learn to read. And art can tell us such a lot about a culture. Simply listening to Wagner, for example, ought to have warned us about our current conflict with Germany, don't you think?" Fritz's odd eyes darted up from his fruit juice at this comment, but he said nothing. "Well, would you like to see the rest of the Academy now, or would you like to settle into your rooms?"

Fr. Jamie and I elected for the tour, but Ari wanted to settle Archie down for the night, and Fritz went with her. I knew he would want to unpack our luggage himself—he didn't trust anyone else with duties he saw as his own.

The classrooms were all in the basement, just three of them. In the first one, over a large fireplace, hung a portrait of Isambard Kingdom Brunel with the steamship *Great Eastern* in the background. "Now that's a grand sight!" I exclaimed on seeing it.

"You're a fan of Mr. Brunel, are you, Mr. McCracken?"

"Yes, Miss Major, I am. As an engineer, he's one of my heroes." I caught Fr. Jamie's eye. He looked singularly disapproving. "Don't you like Isambard Kingdom Brunel, Father?"

Fr. Jamie shrugged. "Och, I like him well enough. But shouldn't there be a portrait to inspire the students with a great moral example?"

"And who would you suggest, Fr. Erikson?" wondered Miss Major primly. "Sir Galahad, perhaps? Better a real man of real accomplishments than a myth."

"St. Margaret, perhaps," suggested Fr. Jamie, "or St. Francis of Assisi, or St. Andrew, or St. Thomas More, or . . . "

"Thank you, Fr. Erikson," said Miss Major with a prim smile, "for all these suggestions. We will have to see what we can do, won't we?"

Feeling glad Ari hadn't been here to hear that exchange, I followed Miss Major out of the first classroom. The first floor also contained the library and Miss Major's office; climbing the stairs, we reached the level where we had enjoyed our refreshments, and which also sported the kitchens and the refectory, a wide, paneled room with a number of trestles down the middle and a high table on a dais at the far end. "That's where Sir Timothy sits, and the faculty, and any guests who might be visiting," explained Miss Major.

The next floor up was the dormitory, and we did not stay long there. Above it were some laboratories a small observatory, and the faculty offices. After that, we climbed a spiral staircase in one of the bartizans and emerged through a narrow door into a stone passageway. It had once been battlemented along one side, but most of the embrasures had been filled in or converted to glazed windows, and a roof now covered our heads; there were frequent trapdoors in the floor.

"This is what the French call a machicoulis," explained our guide. "From here, the castle's defenders could drop large rocks or boiling water on attackers."

"Did Frithoway ever see action?" I wondered.

"No." Miss Major folded her arms across her chest, as if in mild disapproval. "But the Laird was not a popular man. He was always ready to repel attackers."

"Funny that nobody ever attacked, though."

"Not really, Mr. McCracken. You see, an attacker would have to want something, and frankly, Frith has nothing—just a few sheep."

"Not even any trees," I mused, looking out over the maze, a squat chimney rising from the middle of it, and past the wooded grounds to the bare flanks of the hills, darkening now that the sun was truly down.

"I believe there are some trees on the far northern tip of the island," said Miss Major, as if speaking to a dendrologist. "Just a few." She bestirred herself. "Well, you must be wanting to get changed, perhaps bathe. Allow me to show you to your rooms." That was the end of our tour, and a few minutes later I found myself in the room that had been assigned to me, Ari and Archie. It was full of dour portraits, gold candlesticks, and mahogany furniture. A large four-poster bed was spread with slightly harsh sheets for me and Ari, while a smaller bed had been made for Archie. As I entered Ari, sitting in a deep window seat that overlooked the maze, looked up at me and arched her eyebrow inquiringly.

"I'm a little suspicious of this place," I admitted. "They're almost like communists—everything is about its utility value."

"I'm glad to hear you say that. I was beginning to feel uncomfortable myself."

"I think we should probably get out of here as soon as possible. Maybe we can take a short break at Loch Lomond or something before going back to London."

Ari stood and threw her arms about me. "I'm so glad we agree about that, honey," she said.

"Well, I'll have to see Sir Timothy tomorrow morning, which means we stay one more evening. And I have to see if I can find out anything for Birrell. I'm hoping Sir Timothy will take me around his food processing plant. Can you stand being here that long?"

Ari nodded. "Archie and I can go down to the beach and play in the water while you do all that."

And with that resolution in our hearts, we dressed and went down to dinner.

CHAPTER 11
INTO THE MAZE

Sir Timothy had not returned by ten o'clock the following morning. Ari and Fritz took Archie to the beach without me and Fr. Jamie went to visit the academy and sit in on a few classes. I waited hour after hour, turning the pages of my battered copy of Henry Brown's *507 Mechanical Movements*. At last, when the clock outside my door was chiming one o'clock, one of the masters from the Academy knocked at the door to inform me that Sir Timothy was now available. I made my way to Sir Timothy's office. I could hear the distant sound of children singing. It seemed to be a song about arithmetic—school was evidently in session. Sir Timothy's secretary announced me, and I went inside.

"Ah, McCracken!" Sir Timothy LaGrange rose from his seat. A man was sitting across the desk from him, in his middle fifties, smartly dressed with a sharp nose and a slight crease between his eyebrows. "Have you met Herbert Fisher, President of the Board of Education?"

"I haven't." We shook hands—a firm clasp, and a dry hand. Fisher's eyes remained distant.

"Mr. Fisher," explained Sir Timothy, "is hoping to make education in state schools compulsory for everyone in this country, up to the age of fourteen."

"The Education Act," said Fisher in clipped syllables. "It will pass, LaGrange, it will pass. The aim is a thoroughly modern program of education and a thoroughly educated populace. One hundred percent literacy, that's the goal."

"Do you think that's possible?" I wondered. "What if they resist learning?"

Fisher nodded wisely. "Well, you can't educate a chap past his abilities. As for his desires—well, the cane is a powerful persuader, Mr. McCracken."

"Relevance, Mr. Fisher," put in Sir Timothy. "Show them their education is useful, and they'll eat it up." He winked at me. "Engineering—that's it. We need engineers, like Mr. McCracken here. We need scientists."

"I read about a scientist once," I said, "who thought he could bring back the dinosaurs. He was successful."

The crease between Fisher's eyebrows deepened. "I never heard of him. What happened to him?"

"One of the dinosaurs ate him." There was a short, bemused pause, and then Fisher and Sir Timothy laughed.

"Was that one of those stories—what do they call them? Science romance?"

"Or science fiction," I replied to Sir Timothy's question, "yes. But the point of the story was that science alone is not enough—science needs to be used wisely and ethically."

"Yes," harrumphed Fisher, "well, that's all very well in a *story*, I suppose. As for ethics—well, that seems more the province of the Church than the School, don't you think? Some churches, anyway—not . . . " His eyes narrowed as he looked from one to the other of us. Then he stooped to pick up his briefcase. "Anyway, Sir Timothy, I thank you for your hospitality and your introduction to me of this interesting specimen of education. I shall certainly be thinking of you and your academy through the summer as we draft the bill." They shook hands and he nodded to me. "Mr. McCracken," he said, and departed.

Sir Timothy, his lips half-smiling, looked at me as he resumed his seat. Silence grew for a moment then, with a glimmer in his eye, he reached into an inside pocket of his coat and drew out his silver cigarette case. "Cigarette, McCracken?" he asked. "Oh, but I was forgetting—you don't smoke." Snapping the cigarette case shut again, he put it down on the desk. "Don't worry, I won't smoke in your presence!" He sat back in his chair and regarded me benevolently for a moment. "Well, McCracken, here we are—our third encounter. My friends in Chicago would call this 'enemy action,' though I confess to not the least atom of enmity. How about you? Of course, of course, I understand—that's how you feel too. Now, I know what you've been thinking. I ought to tell you that I wasn't actually cheating at cards. Why would I cheat? If I'd won every penny in that room, I still wouldn't have increased my wealth by more than the tiniest fraction. But the game, McCracken—the game! Who was it who said, 'If you would see a man's disposition, watch him gamble, and you will learn more of him in an hour than in seven years' conversation.' I think it was Plato." I didn't think it was Plato, but I said nothing, and naturally the steamroller continued. "I was trying to gauge the people I was playing with, Mr. McCracken, to assess how we could best bring about a reconciliation between the clans. Doesn't that make sense? Yes, I knew you'd see it my way. Well, I'm very busy right now, Mr. McCracken, it's been nice talking with you. I do appreciate honest conversations. Thank you for visiting."

Now was the moment. I had to ask Sir Timothy for permission to visit his plant, and there was a lull in the monologue. "Sir Timothy, you had mentioned . . . "

"Yes, yes, I understand. However, I am very busy at this moment. Important things to be done! People are depending on me. Perhaps we can talk about it this evening at supper?" Standing up, he pumped my hand with vigour. "Thank you for our conversation. I've enjoyed it immensely. I think you and I agree about all this, don't you? And thank you for stopping by."

As he spoke, he walked with me to the door. Opening it, he paused and I was able to interject: "Sir Timothy, we haven't agreed on anything."

"That's what I like about you, McCracken," rejoined Sir Timothy, "your honesty. Well, thank you for this opportunity."

With that, he closed the door, leaving me staring bewilderedly at his secretary. She gave me a watery smile as I wandered through the door and out again.

When I had got back to the room, it was to find Ari, Fritz, and Fr. Jamie deep in conversation. They all looked up at me, questions in their eyes.

"What have you all been talking about?" I wondered.

"Frankly, Cracky, I'm very suspicious," declared Fr. Jamie. "I sat in on a few classes at the Academy this morning, and I felt that the wee ones were being not so much educated as trained, indoctrinated. There was no freedom, no joy in learning. It was all discipline—stand in straight lines, march in time, do what you're told. And all the talk was about being useful—useful to the state. I've never heard so much talk of the economy in a schoolroom. In the upper forms, they were dividing the pupils up—these for the university, these for working in the banks, these for working in the factories, these for secretaries, these for mothers, and so on."

"Seriously? And they didn't mind?"

"They clapped to hear their destinies," lamented Fr. Jamie. "It was as if this was the end of something they'd been hearing for years. One of them said she'd be happy to be a mother so she could provide Britain with more workers. I tell you, Cracky, this is not education. And another thing—there was no Crucifix in the whole place, nor did the masters mention God at all."

"Did you talk to them about all this?"

"Aye, to young McGross. He said religion and education ought to be separate."

"That sounds like what I heard from Sir Timothy and Mr. Fisher just now," I said.

Fr. Jamie became thoughtful. "He also said that a citizen's first loyalty was to the state, not to the Church, not even to the family. Now, he didn't sound like he was fully behind that idea. I couldn't figure out what his honest opinion was, but he seemed to have some misgivings. You can imagine, I told him my own thoughts—that the Church should have a role in education, for otherwise there would be no morality at all in business, in politics, in the world. He looked as if he'd never thought of the matter before, as if it was one of the things he *could not* think about."

"Was there anything else?"

"Some of the masters have made themselves unpopular in Lerwick by poking fun at the vicar of the Anglo-Scottish Kirk there. Now, he's no powerful intellect, you ken, but to be so merciless in your mockery is not a good thing."

"What did you learn from Sir Timothy?" asked Ari.

I shrugged. "He doesn't seem to want to show me around the plant," I told them. "I'm going to have to sneak in under cover of darkness."

Fr. Jamie stared out of the window. "It's in the middle of that maze, Cracky," he observed. "Number One Rule about mazes—never enter at night."

"Always to the right keep," Fritz chimed in. "Your hand on the right wall. You will always the way out find."

I nodded. "I've heard that," I said. "But I think I'll use Tremaux's Algorithm." At the blank stares, I went on, "You know, the algorithm that helps you get through mazes. What on earth did you do when you were children?"

"I read books," said Ari.

"I prayed," said Fr. Jamie.

"I re-enacted historic battles with toy soldiers and how the losing general could have won I calculated," said Fritz, and we all stared at him for a few moments.

"Well, that's all very useful, of course," I said, "especially the toy soldier stuff, but I tried to figure out mathematical solutions to all problems. And I found out about this Pierre Tremaux, who was a French architect. His algorithm was very useful to me when I was a boy. I remember my school trip to London when I was a nipper. We visited Hampton Court, among other places. I got through the maze in five minutes. The other boys were stuck there another half hour. Robbie McTavish never got back, and Mrs. Donaldson sent me in after him."

"Och, I remember that," interjected Fr. Jamie.

"Was he all right?" asked Ari.

"Crying like a baby," I answered, "but he wasn't hurt."

"So, Cracky, how does this algorithm thing work?"

"Well, assuming there's only one entrance and one exit, and that's true of this maze, because there's only one way in or out, and it's there to protect the entrance to the factory, then all you have to do is mark each node, each place where multiple paths connect. If you eliminate dead-ends as you go, you'll get through it in no time. The first rule is, Never go down the same path more than twice. Mark each path, and mark it when you've been down it a second time, and you can keep that rule. The second rule is, Whenever you reach a dead-end, back-track to the last node where there was a fresh path, then mark the dead-end path and take the fresh path."

"What do you mark them with?"

"Anything—different-coloured stones, bread crumbs, chalk signs. Whatever you have."

Reaching into his pocket, Fr. Jamie clapped a pile of coins on the table. "Different denominations of coin?" he suggested.

"Of which there are far too many in this country," Ari remarked drily.

I pored over the pile of silver, copper, even brass, that lay on the table and emptied my own pocket into it. Fritz followed suit. "Perfect," I purred. "These should be easy to tell apart by the light of an electric torch."

Ari regarded the pile with skepticism. "What are all these things?" She stirred the pile with a dubious forefinger. "I've lived here for five months, and I still can't make any sense of it."

"Well, this is a copper." I held one up for her to see. "And this is a tanner, and this is a two-bob bit. This is a half-crown, and this . . ."

"But how does it work?" asked Ari, frowning.

"It's very simple, my dear," replied Fr. Jamie. "There are twelve pennies, or coppers, in a shilling, and twenty shillings, or twenty bob, in a pound."

"So, two-hundred and forty pennies in a pound?" Fr. Jamie and I nodded; Fritz raised his eyebrows—he still couldn't accept it. "Why?" asked Ari.

"Well, let's see." I thought a moment. "In America, you have a hundred cents to the dollar. If you want to pay a half-dollar, you have a coin for it. It you want to pay a quarter of a dollar, you have a coin for it. But what happens when you want to pay a third of a dollar?"

"You pay a quarter, a nickel, and three pennies," answered Ari. "Thirty-three cents."

"Right, but that isn't exactly a third—a third would be thirty-three and a third cents. For us, a third of a pound is eighty pennies, or six shillings and eightpence." I moved six bob, a tanner, and two coppers into a separate pile. "One third of a pound," I declared.

"You could do it like this too," said Fr. Jamie, piling up two half-crowns, two tanners, and two thrup'ny bits.

"Or like this—three two-bob bits and a tanner."

Ari's arms were folded across her chest. "You all are having far too much fun with this," she observed. "Is it designed just to confound foreigners?"

"No, like I say, it's designed for flexibility. We used to have farthings, which were worth a quarter of a penny."

"And even quarter-farthings, if you lived in Ceylon or India," said Fr. Jamie.

"What's this?" Ari held up a brass coin with twelve sides.

"That's worth three pennies. We call it a thrup'ny bit."

"And this?" She had picked up a small silver coin.

"A sixpence, or tanner."

"Which is it?"

"Both—*tanner* is a nickname for sixpence bit. Oh, that's a shilling, or one-bob. That's a two-bob bit, and that half-crown is worth two and six."

"Two and six what?"

"Two shillings and sixpence. That's a half-penny piece, but we pronounce it *haip-nee*. It's really easy when you get used to it."

Ari gave a sigh. "Maybe we'll go somewhere else soon, and I won't have to."

"I'll mark each node I visit with a penny, each new path with a thrup'ny bit, and switch that for a tanner if it proves to be a dead-end. We seem to have most of those, and they'll show up as very different by torchlight." I looked at the maze through the window. "It shouldn't take me much more than ten minutes or so, even at night-time."

I know it's a bit of an anticlimax, but it really was easy to get to the centre of the maze that night, using Tremaux's Algorithm. As dark as it was, my torch picked out a route. I moved swiftly and almost silently, ultimately leaving behind me a trail of sixpence pieces that shone with a moonlight glimmer when I directed the narrow beam of the torch on them. In ten minutes, I stood at the centre of the maze, and before me towered the chimney we had all seen from the castle. It stood forty feet above my head, its bricks dark with night, and beside it was a hut with a single door and no windows. Its roof was higher than I would have expected for its floor-plan. I reached out to press down on the door handle when I heard a clanking sound from within, and ducked around the corner of the hut. The door opened, and two men emerged, chatting with one another in low voices as they headed off through the maze. I returned to the door, eased it open, and looked inside.

Inside was the iron cage of a work elevator, and now I knew why the roof was tall—it housed the gears of the lifting mechanism.

With a shudder and the whirr of an electric motor, the gears moved, and the elevator began to slide down its shaft. I dropped myself onto the roof of the elevator and traveled with it down the shaft until it came to a stop with a bump. Beside me was a small recess in the elevator shaft, within which was a shelf on which rested some tools. I stepped into the recess while another couple of workmen stepped into the elevator and ascended to the surface. When the elevator had risen above my head, I passed under it and into what lay beyond.

What lay beyond amazed and stunned me. I found myself in a wide cavern. Roughly circular, I guessed it to be about five hundred feet in diameter. It had not always been so large; some ancient hands had scooped out extra chambers and then supported the roof with thick, rough-hewn pillars. Sir Timothy had arranged his food processing machinery behind some of these pillars, deep-fat fryers and ovens and pressure canners, all linked one with the other by conveyor belts. The finished products had been crated, the crates stacked along a concrete wharf along with huge bags of potatoes and other roots and vegetables, some of which were open and spilling their contents. But I didn't notice any of this at first. My attention was riveted by the sleek black shape of the submarine moored at the wharf. I couldn't help but note that on the side of its conning tower was painted in white *U57*, and that the ensign that hung from its flagpole was that of the German *Kriegsmarine*.

CHAPTER 12
SPIES AND STALAGMITES

Beside the U-boat stood the dashing figure of its captain, slender and handsome, his *käpitanleutnant*'s uniform slightly disheveled, his chin slightly bristling. He was in earnest conversation with Sir Timothy LaGrange, and from their gestures and glances, I guessed that their conversation focused mostly on the crates being disembarked by a chain of submariners. Already, the stacks of crates on the concrete wharf were head-high.

So, I thought, LaGrange is in league with the Germans. I should have guessed! I have to find out what's in those crates.

Moving cautiously and staying low, I made my way towards the growing stack of crates. At one point, I was close enough to hear the voices of LaGrange and the U-boat captain, but there was too much other noise in the cavern, what with the whirring and clanking of the machinery, the crackling of the deep-fat fryers, and the hum of the ventilators, and I couldn't make out any words other than "re-supply" and "tides" from the German. I moved on towards the crates. There were plenty of things to hide behind—stacks of wood, coils of rope, barrels of oil, and so forth. Soon, I had reached my destination, and now I could hear cheerful German voices jesting with one another. I peered round an oil barrel at the crates.

Each one was stamped in red with a Chinese character, some with two. Taking out my notebook, I carefully copied the characters down, thinking that Ari, with her skill in languages, would be able to make something of them. She could tell me what was in the crates, and that would unlock the secret of the hidden cavern. I resolved to return to the castle, and made my way stealthily back to the elevator, miraculously without being seen.

But that wouldn't last. There were three workers waiting for the elevator, and I couldn't reach it without attracting their attention. They all wore overcoats and hard-hats, and bantered with one another cheerfully as they waited. One of them saw me approaching and nodded a greeting. I nodded back.

Now I was committed.

I joined the group just as the elevator arrived. A hefty man with a bushy beard hauled the door open and we all stepped inside. I could faintly smell warm cooking oil emanating from them. They largely ignored me, talking to one another about Sunday's football match, in which the

LaGrange factory workers were expected to beat the Lerwick fishermen.

"Do ye play?" one of them asked me suddenly.

I shook my head and tapped my leg. "Leg wound," I explained, remembering my time in France.

The man clicked his tongue and shook his head. "Fightin' fer the Sassenach?"

"Aye."

"Same auld story. The Wallace would turn in his grave."

"That he would. That he would!"

The elevator reached the top of the shaft, and we all trooped out into the maze. They seemed to know their way well and went along at a cracking speed. And now I was known to them, I couldn't stop to pick up the coins I'd used as markers. I decided I must return later to retrieve them.

Outside the maze, we parted company. "Wha's like us, eh?" said one.

"Gey few," said one of the others, "an' they're a' deid."

With a gruff nods all around, we went in different directions. I stole through the grounds of the castle, testing the French doors back into the main hall gently and letting myself through without a sound. All about me, the castle seemed to groan and creak, and at each footfall I expected to see the prim and forbidding silhouette of Miss Major before me. But I got up the stairs and through the door of our room without hazard. I closed the door behind me.

Archie was asleep, but Ari sat awake in the rocking chair beside the window. An oil lamp cast a warm glow over her hauntingly beautiful face. She was reading from the volume of Robert Burns she had picked up from a bookseller in Edinburgh, and four hefty volumes were spread out around her. A rosary lay on the bed. I quickly told her what I had discovered in the cavern.

"I'm glad you're back safe," Ari said when I had concluded. "I found that in the library," she added. I had picked up one of the books that lay about her chair. Turning to the title page of one volume, I read:

AN

ETYMOLOGICAL DICTIONARY

OF THE

SCOTTISH LANGUAGE

ILLUSTRATING

THE WORDS IN THEIR DIFFERENT

SIGNIFICATIONS

BY EXAMPLES FROM

ANCIENT AND MODERN WRITERS

BY JOHN JAMIESON, D.D.

FELLOW OF THE ROYAL SOCIETY OF

EDINBURGH

"So it's a dictionary?" I said.

Ari nodded. "It's fascinating. There are a few basic linguistic principles, which I think will be fairly easy to master. For example, in the Scots dialect, you don't round your lips in words like *stone*, which is what gives you *stane*; *go* becomes *gae*, *from frae*. Often, the Scots will drop the final *l* in a word, so that *ball* becomes *baw*, *salt saut*, and so on. Then there's the velar fricatives—"

"The wha'?"

"Fricatives—you know, when you make a continual sound by friction in a narrow opening at the point of articulation, like the *f* in English or the *ch* in Scots words like *loch* or *nicht*." I must have looked perplexed, because she smiled again, shut the book, and said, "Ye've git a letter, cam' fer ye wheil ye were awa'." She pronounced each word perfectly but in her American accent.

"A letter! Where?"

She pointed. "It's on the window-sill."

I looked at the window; there was no letter. But on closer examination, I saw it all right—on the outside of the glass, weighed down by a stone—or a *stane*, perhaps. The drop to the bushes below was vertical and about fifty feet. I couldn't see well—it was long after midnight—but I thought the wall was pretty sheer and offered relatively few hand- and foot-holds.

"Who on earth could have put it there?" I wondered, raising the casement and retrieving the letter. It was certainly addressed to me.

"I don't know," admitted Ari, "but I didn't hear a thing, except when whoever it was tapped on the window. That gave me a fright. And when I got to the window, there was no one to be seen. He must be good—or she."

On the piece of paper were neatly printed the words *Laird's Leap, 4 a.m. J. B*. "J. B.—Johnnie Birrell!" I exclaimed. "He must have caught up with us. I wonder what he wants to talk about?"

"Do you think he'll be able to help us?"

"I don't know." I showed her the Chinese characters I'd copied down. "Can you tell me what these signs mean?"

Ari held the note up to the light, her brow creased. "I'd need to look at some books," she admitted doubtfully. "Perhaps they have them in the library here. I'll check tomorrow morning."

I was a little belligerent at this. "Don't you just know? I mean, you're supposed to be a wizard with languages."

Ari's patient smile betrayed at once her impatience and massive self-control. "There are somewhere between five and seven thousand characters in modern Chinese. I can't know everything." She lowered the paper into her lap. "So Sir Timothy is working with the Germans."

"Yes. I have no idea what he's doing, but I think the contents of those crates are important. I'd better let Birrell have some copies of those Chinese characters when I go to see him."

So Ari copied the Chinese characters down for herself and gave me my notebook back. An hour later, I once more sneaked out of the castle and struck out towards Laird's Leap.

The half-moon hung low on the horizon, spilling its silver into the sea below, when I finally made it to the wind-swept cliff-top. The shadows were strange and blue, and I could hear the breakers dashing themselves against the foot of the cliff. Peering over the edge at the foamy waters below, I felt the wind buffeting my hair and flattening my clothes against me. My stomach churned like the waves to look down all that way and into practically nothing. The chaos of the ocean.

"It wasn't a slow death, you know," said a voice, and I turned in surprise to find Birrell standing slightly behind me on the clifftop. "Laird Alastair jumped in January. The water was icy-cold. His body would have gone into shock immediately, and he would have lost consciousness."

"What a lot of grisly things you know, Birrell," I said, shaking his hand. "How have you been?"

"Well," answered Birrell. "As well as can be expected, anyway. Must say, old chap, it's fairly difficult keeping up with you."

"You've been following me?" A light suddenly went on somewhere inside me. "Then it was you Father saw on the ferry?" Birrell nodded. "And that I saw in Edinburgh, coming out of the church?"

Another nod. "I should apologize for all that, old chap—should have warned you I'd be following you. You know, just to make sure you didn't get into too much trouble."

"Were you on the train too?" I asked.

"I was. And I think that requires another apology. You see, Damlich was actually after me, not you. You can probably appreciate his surprise when he saw you!"

I gave an ironic grin. "His day was full of surprises."

"Yes. Well, he's currently experiencing all his surprises from a hospital bed back in London, under guard."

"Will he be shot as a spy?"

"Probably," answered Birrell in a nonchalant way. "That's part of the risk you take in this job. Afraid it's rather necessary. That Mata Hari woman the French shot last year—well, she probably cost the lives of fifty or sixty thousand of our boys. But who knows? Perhaps Damlich will get lucky. Perhaps this time the War really will be over by Christmas. He may get away with it." He led me away from the edge of the cliff, asking, "So, have you been able to find out anything about Sir Timothy's activities?"

For the second time that night, I related what I'd seen in the cavern and handed him the page of my notebook with the Chinese characters. "Thanks for this, old chap. See what I can find out. But the U-boat is enough for me—that proves he's up to no good. Regardless of what's in those crates, we have to stop him."

"Is there anybody who can help us?" I asked. "Or are we all alone in this?"

"Well, there's a platoon of the Gordon Highlanders billeted in Lerwick."

"That's a fortunate coincidence!" I responded.

"Not exactly." Birrell gave a lop-sided grin. "When I knew where we were headed, I pulled a few strings. Thought we might need back-up."

"That's very helpful. When do you think you can get them here?"

"Probably no sooner than nine, I should think. Could you delay the U-boat a bit?"

"There's always a way of delaying a ship," I answered. "I might be able to rig up a small bomb and do some damage with that. My guess is that the U-boat will have to leave about nine o'clock to catch the tide."

"If you could arrange for a small explosion, say, in a torpedo tube, at about eight, that should do the trick. Do you need any explosives?"

I shook my head. "Ari should have what I need."

We parted company. Birrell had a small motor-launch hidden along the coast, and he would use that to get back to Lerwick, while I returned to the castle, arriving a little after five. That would give me about an hour of sleep, so I lay down on top of the covers rather than getting in beside Ari. I didn't dare set my alarm clock—I wanted to be able to sneak out and through the maze without waking anyone up. I drifted into sleep and out of it for a while, then snapped awake when the grey light from outside was just filtering through the curtains. I looked at my watch.

It was almost seven o'clock!

I leaped from the bed, waking Ari in the process.

"What's going on?" she asked in a bleary voice.

"Where are your boots?" I asked. "I need your dynamite."

She pointed. "What for?"

I found her boots, swiveled the heel of the left one on its pivot, and extracted the tiny stick of dynamite Ari kept there. It was a nice gadget that she'd picked up in New York a few years previously. "I'm trying to delay the U-boat from leaving," I said, "but I think I'm late. Pray for me."

"I will," she said, sitting up in bed and crossing herself as I opened the door and shut it softly behind me.

The castle was perfectly still, and the sunlight had not yet penetrated into the interior. The dynamite in one pocket, my revolver in the other, my boots in one hand, I tiptoed, stocking-footed, down the stairs and towards the French doors.

"Going somewhere, Mr. McCracken?"

I spun round. Miss Major stood in the shadows, a thin ribbon of light falling across her narrow face.

"Just going for my morning constitutional, Miss Major," I said, smiling. "I didn't want to wake anyone up."

"Of course not." The prim smile pressed itself onto her lips for a moment. "Sir Timothy is also awake this morning, and wonders if you would be kind enough to call upon him."

"Certainly—just as soon as I get back from my walk."

"I think now would be best," Miss Major insisted.

"As you say. Anything important?"

Her smile was not quite so prim this time. "I think it's better if Sir Timothy explains to you in person. Don't worry, Mr. McCracken—I'll be there too."

"You've no idea how that fills me with confidence, Miss Major," I said, quickly slipping my feet into my shoes and tying the laces.

Miss Major and I walked together back up the stairs and paused outside Sir Timothy's office. His secretary was not there, but three of the schoolmasters, including McGross, sat in the anteroom. When Miss Major knocked, Sir Timothy's voice called, "Come!" and we went inside.

"Mr. McCracken!" beamed LaGrange, rising from his desk and greeting me with a handshake. "Sit down—do, please." We both took our seats on opposite sides of the desk. Miss Major sat off to the side.

"What can I do for you, LaGrange?" I asked. Something stirred in the shadows behind LaGrange's desk, and I saw that Fr. Kerr was there too.

"What can you do for me? I like that—I do, I really like that. I do enjoy your honesty, Mr. McCracken, and I must also say, I like your helpfulness. You've always been helpful, every time we've met. I remember our first meeting—what my Chicago friends would call *happenstance*. A most pleasant meeting, though I think you derived a misunderstanding about me from it. Still, most pleasant, most pleasant indeed. Then we met in Edinburgh. That would be *coincidence*, according to my Chicago friends." He wagged an admonishing forefinger at me. "I think you misunderstood me again, Mr. McCracken. But of course, I can't blame you for that. It's your honesty, you see, your honesty. You can't help that, and it's a virtue, after all. Of course it is. A virtue. And now we are here. Our third meeting, what my friends would call *enemy action*. But that can't be completely accurate, can it, Mr. McCracken? Because you just offered to help me. And enemies don't offer to help. Friends help one another, loyal friends. Shall we call it *friendly action* then, Mr. McCracken, or perhaps *loyal action*? I think so. I've always liked you, as you know, and I'd like to give back to you what you have given me. Your help. I'd like to return to you something you lost."

Sir Timothy LaGrange held his clenched fist over the table and, opening it, dropped a pile of pennies, tanners, and threepenny bits on the desktop.

"You left these in the maze last night, Mr. McCracken." LaGrange's eyes narrowed. "I thought you might want them back." He nodded to Miss Major, who rose from her seat and opened the office door. The three schoolmasters from outside, including Charlie McGross, entered. Each carried a Luger.

"I think, Mr. McCracken," said Sir Timothy, sitting back in his chair and pressing his fingertips together, "that perhaps my friends in Chicago were right after all."

CHAPTER 13
THE STEEL PRISON

I leaped instantly to my feet. "I know what you're up to, LaGrange," I said. Before I could add to my comment, two of the schoolmasters stepped up to me. One of them seized my arms so I couldn't move while the other frisked me quickly and removed the Scott-Webley revolver from my jacket pocket, the dynamite from the other, my wallet and loose change. He placed them all on the desk in front of LaGrange, then the two of them retired to flank the door. They stood at attention, like well-trained soldiers.

LaGrange popped open the Scott-Webley's cylinder and emptied the rounds onto the desktop. They made a metallic clatter and one rolled onto the floor. "I very much doubt that, Mr. McCracken. I know exactly what Kapitän Steinbrinck and I discussed last night, and I know you could learn nothing from it. Mr. McGross." McGross stepped smartly forward, clicking his heels in a very military fashion. "Please go and find Mrs. McCracken and that charming little boy and bring them here. The priest and the German cook too." McGross gave a nod that was a lot like a salute, wheeled about, and strode from the room.

LaGrange snapped the cylinder back in place and set the revolver down on the desk. "I think families will very soon be a thing of the past, Mr. McCracken. What do you think?"

"I think that's insane," I retorted.

LaGrange gave a tight smile. "That's what I'd expect you to think—honest, Mr. McCracken, but not really forward-thinking. You're stuck with traditions. You need to break away from them, live a modern life. This family loyalty, for instance. What could be more misplaced than that? Let's face it, Mr. McCracken, most mothers and fathers are what you might call unintelligent. And the poor are incapable of raising children properly—they haven't the means. They should never have had children in the first place. The Government can look after children—educate them, feed them, minister to their health—better than parents can. If the Catholic Church won't abandon its stupid trust in families, then the Government ought to do something about it."

"The family is the basis of a healthy society," I replied. "The Government could never replace it—replace love with bureaucracy? Never. But what's the point of arguing with you, LaGrange? Your money has warped your mind. You're nothing but a fake—a fake Catholic and a fake philanthropist. Everything about you is a lie, isn't it?"

LaGrange laughed and clapped his hands slowly. "Oh, very good, Mr. McCracken, very good indeed. If I had a bleeding heart instead of a brain, I might fall for all these appalling weaknesses. No, McCracken, your ways are over, your Church is virtually dead. The gates of hell do seem to have prevailed over it after all. Better line up with the Devil now. At least we'll be on the winning side." He paused and looked at me closely. "Oh, have I offended you?" he asked.

"What does that matter?" I demanded. "You're nothing but a faithless traitor."

LaGrange raised his eyebrows and shook his head. "Harsh words, harsh words, Mr. McCracken," he said. "Have no fear for me, though. When history judges me, I trust it will use more useful criteria than outdated morality and an idiotic loyalty to inefficient biological relationships. The world has changed, and what does not change will be destroyed—Church and family." He considered me for a few moments placidly. "Since Mr. McGross seems to be taking his time finding your . . . well, for want of a better word, your *family*, we have a few moments to spend. I don't mind talking to you—honestly, of course. As a matter of fact, Mr. McCracken, I was baptized a Catholic, and Catholicism provided me a useful cover for my operations. The British are always suspicious of Catholics, and if they're suspicious of that, they don't pry into too much else. 'What can you expect? He's a papist.' You can hear it, can't you? As for philanthropy, well, that's a useful cover for moving around large amounts of money. Have you ever considered, Mr. McCracken, that most philanthropists don't really love anybody? They love ideas. They love the idea of ending world hunger, or of providing shoes for African children, or of founding libraries for the poor. Above all, they love the idea of themselves as generous without the inconvenience of actually meeting hungry or shoeless or illiterate people. All they have to do is occasionally sign checks, giving away a lot of what they already have plenty of. No, Mr. McCracken, it was a perfect cover for me."

"So what *are* you up to?" I asked.

"Oh no, Mr. McCracken." The finger wagged back and forth again. "You won't draw me into talking about my plans. I know that's the sort of thing your adversaries always do, but they all failed. I don't think you'll escape, but what if you did, possessed with knowledge of my plans? Now, if you'd come to Frith with an *honest* intention, we could have had long conversations about all these things. You might even have been persuaded to abandon your silly, old-fashioned ideas and join my organization. But in fact you came here to spy on me. That was very disloyal of you. No, I've discussed your situation with Captain Steinbrinck, and he wants to take you to Germany for interrogation. You have been a minor inconvenience to them, and they would like more information."

"So you're working for the Germans?"

"*With*, Mr. McCracken, not *for*." He stopped, looked at me closely, and then said, "Well, look at that, Mr. McCracken. You made me reveal something I didn't wish to reveal. Honest, helpful, and clever too. You are full of virtues, Mr. McCracken—full of them! What a pity that virtues won't be in fashion very much longer. Or if they are, they'll be wholly redefined." His smile broadened. "I can't resist telling you— that's what the schools are all about. But enough of my plans. Ah, here is Mr. McGross!"

The door opened, but it was not McGross. It was another of the schoolmasters. "Sir, Canning says he heard gunfire in the area of the West Gate."

LaGrange and Miss Major exchanged glances. "Where is Mr. McGross?"

"I don't know, sir."

"We'll have to get McCracken out of here," Miss Major told him. "No time to lose."

Fr. Kerr leaped from his seat and into the light. "We must get him into the submarine at once. We cannot lose our prize!"

They pushed me at gunpoint out onto the landing. My mind was whirling. Where were Ari and Archie, Fr. Jamie and Fritz? And where were Johnnie Birrell and the Gordon Highlanders? As if in answer to my mental question, a gunshot rang out from somewhere in front of the castle. It was followed by the rat-tat-tat of a Lewis machine-gun.

LaGrange grabbed a handful of my sleeve and jerked me along the way. "Don't worry, Mr. McCracken. You can't pin anything on me so long as you don't know what it is I'm doing. I'm safe—safe because I'm rich."

We sped lightly down the stairs and turned right to leave the castle and make for the maze.

"I suppose you'd like to use your French algorithm, Mr. McCracken." LaGrange was pushing me through the entrance and into the maze. "As it happens, I know the way very well indeed."

A left, a right, a long straight bit and then another right. More shots behind us—the tight cracks of the Lee Enfields mixed in with the echoing reports of the Gewehr 98s. We reached the centre of the maze, with the chimney and the little hut beside it. Miss Major opened the door for me.

"After you, Miss Major," I said.

"Oh, don't be facile, Mr. McCracken," she replied, and gave me a shove.

The U-boat commander awaited us on the wharf, two submariners armed with Lugers standing at attention behind him. No one else was in sight, and the submarine engines hummed. I could smell the diesel.

"Ah, Herr McCracken," said the U-boat captain. "You see, you have been recognized, and you have been captured."

I waved a hand at the Luger-toting schoolmasters behind me. "You have me at a disadvantage, *Herr Kapitän.*"

"Please excuse my ill manners, Herr McCracken. After many weeks at sea, one forgets." He gave a curt bow and a click of the heels. "*Kapitänleutnant* Otto Steinbrinck, at your service."

"Forgive me, Captain, if I'm a little suspicious of your service," I said. "I've seldom enjoyed the service of folks I've met at gunpoint."

"Ach yes," replied Steinbrinck, "the famous Scottish sense of humour. This I have heard said, Herr McCracken, that a Scottish joke is no laughing matter."

"I've heard the same of German jokes," I replied.

The smile frozen onto his lips didn't thaw at all. "Ach so," he said. "Then we may with humour altogether dispense and speak plainly, like adults."

"You first. I expect you'll want to justify sinking civilian ships."

The corner of Steinbrinck's mouth pressed into a humourless smile. "Perhaps, Herr McCracken, you would like in turn the use of civilian ships for military purposes to justify? In total war, there will be—what is word?—collateral damage." He raised his hand to his mouth to stifle a yawn. "This conversation is very pleasant, Herr McCracken," he said, "but much business we have to conduct, and my orders regarding you are very clear."

"Are you going to torture me?" I demanded. "Is that what they teach in the *Allgemeine Kriegsschule* nowadays?"

"Ah, there you go again with those Scottish jokes that are not so funny," said Steinbrinck. "In the *Allgemeine Kriegsschule* many things they teach, Herr McCracken, but the most important is to follow orders. And my orders are to take you to Danzig and then continue with our operations against enemy ships—both military and civilian, with no distinction to be made. I must to that return with speed, Herr McCracken, and play my part in the most assured victory to come. I can afford no time to torture Scotch men who tell bad jokes."

"Scotch is a drink," I pointed out, "not a person."

"From what I have heard, there is in the Scotch so much Scotch that the difference between them is negligible." His shoulders shook for a moment with silent laughter. "You see, Herr McCracken, a German joke is a laughing matter after all!" He regained control of his shoulders and said, "Danzig I think you will like. You will appreciate the ways they have of extracting information from reluctant *Scotchmen*." Turning to one of the seamen, he snapped: "*Einliefen ihn auf das Boot.*"

"*Jawohl, Herr Kapitän!*" barked one of the seamen, and stepping forward he pushed me towards the gangplank.

"And you, Sir Timothy?" said Steinbrinck, as I started climbing the ladder to the top of the conning tower, "will you accompany us?"

"Forgive me, Captain," answered LaGrange, "but I think this will be easy enough for me to explain. A few bribes in high places and I'll be fine. But thank you for your concern—thank you! It's so pleasant to talk to you, always!"

"*Alles ist gut*," replied Steinbrinck, shooting out a gloved hand to shake with Sir Timothy. "Then, with great respect, I shall say, *Auf wiedersehen.*" He turned and followed us into the conning tower, then through a hatch and down into the cramped belly, all dials and valves and bare electric lights, of the submarine. It smelled of sweat and oil.

At a sharp intake of breath, I turned around, and looked into the face of a young seaman in a white jacket. He was about nineteen years old, and there was something familiar about his face, but I couldn't say anything. The Lugers were most persuasive.

I was escorted through the ship into the bows, where one of my guards opened the door of a small cabin or a large closet—I couldn't tell which. Once I was inside, they slammed the door, and I heard the bolt falling into place.

The steel prison in which I found myself was uninspiring. It was lit by a single naked light bulb, and contained nothing, except me.

Shortly afterwards, I heard the thump of the engines increase their rhythm, and I knew we were on our way to Germany.

It's hard to say how long I sat in that closet. By my watch, almost two days passed; but forty-eight hours in a closet seems like far more than forty-eight hours. I couldn't move more than a single pace in either direction, I couldn't sleep for anxiety. The Germans didn't mistreat me—they left that for the authorities over to whom I would be handed when we reached Danzig.

I tried to pray—you can fit a lot of rosaries into forty-eight hours if you've nowhere to go. I think, at first, I expected to hear God's voice, telling me that all would come right, that He would open the steel door for me and show me how to get out and defeat LaGrange at whatever he was doing. But God did not speak, and as the hours passed I grew more and more afraid—not for myself, but for Ari and Archie. What would LaGrange do to them? I wondered. Not much, I knew, if he wanted to ingratiate himself back into good society; but if I knew Ari, she wouldn't give up. She would hound LaGrange until he was behind bars—and a rich enemy is a dangerous one. I yearned to break out of my confinement and go seeking her; but the door would not budge and, if it did, I had nowhere to go—I was in a submarine among thirty-five hostile souls, probably a couple of hundred feet under the waters of the North Sea. And at that thought, I'd pray another rosary. Even if God doesn't answer me, I thought, I know He's there. One by one, the beads passed through my fingers.

As I say, the longest forty-eight hours of my life had passed, when something different happened.

The door opened, and a young seaman entered. He shut the door again and leaned against it. It was the young man I had seen on entering the U-boat, who had seemed somehow familiar to me.

"Herr McCracken," he said, "I am *Mechanikermaat* Helmut Bauer."

"Nice to meet you," I said with some irony.

He looked around the little room for inspiration, but found nothing. "My name," he said, "do you . . . I cannot say *wissen* in England."

"*Know*?" I suggested.

"*Ja!* Know. You know my name, Herr McCracken?"

"Helmut Bauer?" I said. "I know someone called Bauer."

"*Ja*, Herr McCracken," said the young man. "Fritz Bauer. He is my father."

"You're Fritz's son!" I cried, knowing now where I had seen those features before. Then I realized I should be a lot quieter, and whispered, "I knew Fritz had family who were still in Germany."

Helmut looked as if he were counting in his head for a moment, and then he understood. He said, "My mother, she wants to join my father, but travel it is . . . *schwer*, very hard. She can not join my father. Now I help you."

"You—help me?" I said. "How?"

Helmut opened the door a crack and peeped out. Then he shut it and pressed his back against it again. "Now," he said, "*das Boot*—it is above the water. You understand?" I nodded. "I am *Mechanikermaat*—I care for torpedoes, *ja*?" Again, I nodded. "My job is, I clean torpedo tubes. For this, I must open the outer doors. But in *fünf Minuten*—in five minutes, that is, five minutes after I leave here—" he looked at his watch to be certain, "I must leave torpedo room. It is—how is it in England?—*Ich muss den Wasser besuchen.*" I must have looked puzzled at this, because he became almost frantic. "It is what I must do, all mans do it, in *Badezimmer*. You know what is *Badezimmer*?"

"Bathroom?" I guessed.

"*Ja! Ja!* Bathroom! *Ist gut.* I go to the bathroom. And when I go, torpedo room, she is empty."

I dared not say anything. He seemed to be offering me very much indeed.

"Torpedo tube," Helmut went on, "is big enough a man can get inside." He cracked the door and looked out again, then looked back at me. "You will need *das Beiboot*." He saw my total incomprehension. "*Das Beiboot*? You know what is *das Beiboot*? *Das Boot*—you know? But *wenig, wenig—schmal*."

"Small boat," I said. "Dinghy?"

"Dinghy?" Helmut's lip curled, as if he thought the word unfitting for so noble a vessel. "Maybe yes, maybe no. The small boat she is strapped to *das Deck* in front of . . . of *Kommandoturm*."

"Conning tower?" I suggested.

"Maybe yes, maybe no," answered Helmut with a shrug. "Leave *das Beiboot* on the land. We shall need it back, Herr McCracken."

"Do you know where we are?" I asked.

"We are beside the coast of *Belgien*."

I smiled. "I'll leave the boat on the beach," I assured him. "Thank you, Mechanic's Mate Bauer."

He thrust out his hand to me. "*Auf Wiedersehen*, Herr McCracken." We shook hands. "When next you my father see, please to tell him, *Ich habe ihn lieb. Treffen wir uns wieder am Kriegsende.* Ask him to . . . ask him, *Ora pro me.*"

He made me repeat the message several times, until he was confident I had memorized it.

Helmut was gone a second later.

CHAPTER 14
IN THE DRINK

I waited five minutes—which seemed longer even than the forty-eight hours previous to it—then pushed the door open and made sure there was no one in either direction. I headed swiftly, and without looking back, along the narrow passageway towards the bows. In a few seconds, I found myself in a tight chamber with an arched ceiling. It was a miniature cathedral of chains, valves, gauges, and pistons, its aisles composed of rolling racks where the torpedoes were cranked in before firing. And, directly ahead of me were the twin circular breech-doors that covered the firing tubes.

I knew how they worked. It was a pneumatic system. The tubes were flooded from outside, then the torpedoes were pushed out by pressurized air. If he were lucky, the captain of the victim ship would spot air-bubbles among the waves, and know to take evasive action. But that was rare. The muzzle doors, which were the outer doors through which the torpedo was fired, were operated by a rotating handle.

With a quick, quiet prayer to Our Lady Undoer of Knots, one of Fritz's special devotions,

I rotated the muzzle door handle until it would turn no more. Then I stepped over to the breech door, spun the handle, and pulled it open. Immediately, the echoing noise of the sea bounced around the hollow chamber, and I could smell the salt. Snatching a glance over my shoulder, I climbed into the tube. It was snug, but I could move. But of course I couldn't turn around and close the breech door behind me. That meant it was only a matter of seconds before someone discovered the door open. I pulled myself along the tube, inch by inch. A blast of cold, salty spray filmed my face. Ahead of me, the circle of grey light grew bigger and bigger, until my head emerged into the air.

Immediately, the bows of the submarine dipped, and seawater gushed into the torpedo tube—and into my lungs. I coughed, spluttered, and choked. I almost vomited. Behind me, I heard the water spattering over the steel floor of the torpedo room.

Fear seized me. I grabbed the rim of the muzzle and hauled myself out of the tube. Rotating myself about, I sat in the opening and reached up to see what I could grab. A ridge running along the hull, near the deck, gave me enough purchase, and I heaved myself upwards.

So far, I had been blessed. Helmut might have come back to the torpedo room, in which case he would quietly shut the breech door and, later, the muzzle door, and return everything to normal. But if anyone else entered—

At that moment, I heard a raised voice through the torpedo tube, and the muzzle door began to close on me. I pushed with my feet, dragged myself with my fingers, and felt the wet metal of the deck under the palm of my hand just as the muzzle door closed with a *clang* below me. Levering myself up with one hand, I grabbed the gunwale cable with the other, steadying myself as the bows plunged once more. For a moment, I was up to my waist in freezing water.

No one was on deck. As the seawater drained from it in frothing rills, I scrambled towards the dinghy, which was exactly where Helmut had said it would be. Quickly, I loosed the buckles and pushed the dinghy towards the edge of the deck.

"Halt!" came a strident voice from above me.

Kapitänleutnant Steinbrinck looked down on me from the conning tower and in his hand was—what else?—a Luger.

I straightened, the wind and spray buffeting me, it seemed, from all directions. "If you shoot me, Captain, then whatever information you think I have will be lost."

Steinbrinck nodded. "*Das ist gut*, Herr McCracken," he said. "I have my orders. You understand, I cannot let you escape—my orders forbid it. *Nein*, Herr McCracken, you must either return to the submarine, or else be shot and disappear from history. One way or another, Germany will win—as usual."

I glanced quickly down towards my feet. The dinghy needed just a little shove with my toe to topple over into the choppy waves of the North Sea. I could see the grey coastline with the slender finger of a lighthouse raised as if in admonition not two hundred yards away.

But the Captain seemed to understand my thoughts. "Do not do it, Herr McCracken," he said. "The lighthouse, it looks close. You will freeze to death in these waters, much more quickly than you expect. Before you swam a few strokes, your arms would cease to obey you, and you will feel like lead in the water. You will begin to feel comfortable and carefree, as if the world and all its problems did not matter—and then the end is very near, for that will be your last experience before the cold takes you. And if you get into the dinghy, it will be a very easy matter to shoot you. Once again, Herr McCracken, Germany wins."

But before I could reply, Steinbrinck's eye caught something off the bows. Before he could do anything, the boom of a large-calibre gunshot crashed through the sound of the wind and the spray. He raised his hand in surprise and took a step backwards.

I couldn't look at what he had seen, for at that moment a particularly high wave struck the bows of *U-57*, and seawater crashed along the deck in a roiling mass of white. For a moment, the icy water swirled about my waist. It picked me up, threw me against the conning tower, and bounced me into the sea.

The shock was terrific. I couldn't have been colder, if I had been suddenly encased in an iceberg. I turned over and over, in slow motion, flailing with my arms and legs. The water churned all about me as the submarine plunged past. Eddies caught me and twirled me around, and all the time something huge pressed against my lungs and I could draw no air into them.

Then my head broke the surface, and I gasped as I sucked in the sweet sea air. The submarine's wake caught me and tossed me up and down, and I saw a series of confused images whirling about me: the sleek black shape of *U-57*, surging away from me through the waves, the grey coastline with the lighthouse, somehow at a crazy slant, and the narrow V of another boat.

Then I dropped beneath the surface once again, sucked under by the churning of the submarine's double screws. I struck out with my arms, but they were sluggish, as if made of lead, and for a few moments, I was dragged backwards. The cold soaked into my body, and I found my arms would barely move. I struggled frantically at first, and then more feebly; but my body refused to obey.

God help me! I thought, as I was dragged steadily further under the water.

And then that dreadful force released me, and I was aware that I was moving, once again without any volition. I broke the surface, gagging, sucking in air and thanking God for my deliverance.

I couldn't see the submarine, but I could see the coastline.

I must swim for it, I thought.

My arms moved slowly. One of them rose from the steely waters, dipped in, scooped. But my body didn't move. It was as if I were trying to fly through slowly setting concrete.

Ari. I focused on Ari. She would need me. My arms moved mechanically, but slowly, slowly. I was going nowhere. And I began to wonder if there was really anything I could do after all. Ari, I thought, was a capable woman. She could look after herself, and after Archie. And I wouldn't have to go to all this effort. I could just wait here and rest. The world, the War, LaGrange, all the problems, seemed very far away, like a distant echo in a deep valley.

Something caught me by the scruff of the neck and hauled me, dripping, into the air. I was cast down upon something hard, choking. The world faded to black . . .

* * *

When I awoke, I did not know where I was, nor could I remember, no matter how hard I tried, what had been happening to me. I could remember a ship, a narrow tunnel that shone like steel, Sir Timothy's face, and oddly enough, Fr. Kerr, like a grim shadow. I was under covers in a bed, but I shivered uncontrollably, though I was no longer cold.

No longer cold—that stirred another memory. I remembered darkness and icy cold all around me. But what was the connection? I struggled to remember, but nothing came.

Opening my eyes, I saw I lay in a small cabin with grey walls. I was covered with many layers of sheets and woolen blankets, and my head rested upon a firm pillow of coarse linen. The room swayed from side to side, and I could hear the mechanical throbbing of a ship's engines.

I pushed myself upright and scanned my surroundings. Obviously I was in a ship, under full steam somewhere. The question was, whose ship? The cabin was small, with a single circular porthole and one steel door with a large round handle. I wore long underwear and shirt, but nothing else; neatly folded clothes sat on a small dresser, and these I put on. They were my own, washed and pressed. Before I could slip my feet into my shoes, the handle spun and the door opened. A man in the uniform of a Royal Navy officer stepped in. The gold braid indicated he was a lieutenant.

"*Guten Tag, mein Herr*," he said, closing the door with a soft click behind him.

"I'm not German," I replied. I found I had more difficult than usual forming my words. And what was my name? Never mind—it would come.

"Not German?" I shook my head. "Well, we could see from your clothing that you weren't a member of the crew, but there weren't any identifying papers about you."

No," I said, "they took them away . . . " I stopped. I couldn't tell if I had said anything at all.

"Take it slowly," said the naval officer. "We fished you out of the North Sea off the coast of Belgium. You're suffering the after-effects of hypothermia: shivering, slurred speech, low pulse rate, probably memory loss."

I gave a sluggish nod. "Some of it," I said, my tongue thick, "is coming back."

"You were saying something about your identification papers."

I summoned up all my effort and said with great deliberation, "The captain of the U-boat took them away when he captured me."

"Captured you?" The lieutenant's words were uttered without any emotion at all. He was playing a very reserved game. I explained how I had been captured, and how I had escaped. I found my memory was returning, though sometimes the officer couldn't follow my story and asked me to repeat myself. Other than that, his face didn't change one bit while my story unfolded, and he took notes. At the end of it he flipped his notebook closed and said, "Thank you for your account. I shall signal the Admiralty to confirm your identity, Mr. McCracken. Meanwhile, I'd ask you to confine yourself to quarters here. You are on board His Majesty's torpedo-boat *Thunderer*, and I'm her captain, Lieutenant John Manning. Our assignment is to clear this sector of the North Sea of mines laid by German U-boats. We pulled you out of the water after we opened fire on *U-57* yesterday afternoon."

"Did you sink her?"

"Regrettably, no. We exchanged fire, but neither got any hits. Then the blighter dived. Can you believe her captain actually waved to me?"

"Actually, I can." At least Helmut had survived the encounter, I thought.

A signal came back from the Admiralty shortly afterwards, and I was given liberty of the ship, but not for long. There must have been something else in the cable from London, for the *Thunderer* turned her head about and steamed for England at once. Soon, we were nosing along the River Medway, to finally moor at Chatham Dockyard.

And there, at the bottom of the gangplank, was a knot of people evidently waiting for me: Birrell was among them, and Fritz, and Fr. Jamie and, my heart soaring to see them, Ari and Archie. With them was a heavy-set man in a captain's uniform with a monocle fixed into his right eye.

Archie's feet beat a rapid tattoo on the gangplank as he rushed up to me. I swung him up and hugged him close. Ari joined the embrace and we had a few moments of family time while the others stayed at a discreet distance.

"I've been so worried for you," whispered Ari.

"And I for you," I answered. "But God didn't abandon us. And as for you, young Archie," I added, "you look like you've grown a foot in the couple of days Daddy's been on that boat!"

"Actually, Daddy," said Archie, giving the vessel an appraising glance from stem to stern, "it's a destroyer."

"What?"

"It's a destroyer. Look—guns."

I looked at Ari in amazement, then turned back to Archie. "What's the difference?" I asked him.

Archie gave a nonchalant shrug. "Boats are small. Destroyers have guns."

I hugged him closer. "I'll make an engineer of you yet, you young rapscallion!"

"Actually," muttered Archie, "I'm a boy."

Laughing, we all bundled into the Daimler, but as Fritz cranked the engine, I took him aside. "Fritz," I said, "could I have a word, please?" I took him aside, while the others talked, and said quietly, "I met someone you know the other day."

"Ja, Herr McCracken?" Fritz's eyebrows flew upwards from his strange eyes.

"When we were all split up the other day, I was captured by LaGrange and imprisoned for a couple of days in a U-boat, *U-57*. One of the crewmen helped me escape. I think you know him: Helmut Bauer."

Fritz drew in a sharp breath. "You met my son?" he croaked.

"Yes," I replied. "He's well, I think—I don't know if he got into trouble for helping me escape. He wanted me to tell you something, which I've repeated to myself many times, but I think I'll probably get it wrong anyway: *Ich lieben ihn, und treffen wir und wiener im ende der Krieg.*"

Fritz's eyes shone with tears. "Your German grammar, Herr McCracken," he said, sorrow and joy playing in his face, "it is as poor as my English grammar. But *dankeschön*! Poor Helmut! If only I could have got my wife and children out of Germany before the War began!"

"You'll see them again soon, Fritz—Helga and all fourteen of them!"

"I hope so, Herr McCracken." With a wistful smile, he bent to the crank once more, and before long we were underway.

"McCracken," said Birrell, "have you met C?" I shook hands with the monocled captain. "This is the head of the Secret Service Bureau."

"As a matter of fact," C corrected him, "my name is Cumming—all this initial letter stuff is just a load of balderdash. And the Secret Service Bureau doesn't exist. I'm just a retired captain." His monocle flashed as he turned to me. "Yes, a retired captain who shares an interest with you, Mr. McCracken—fast cars, motor-boats, and aeroplanes. I was a founder member of the Aero Club."

"Really!" I enthused. "Then we'll have lots to talk about!"

Shortly after that, we were all in the study of our flat in London, Fritz pouring drinks all round as I told them of my adventures.

"So," I said, sipping my whisky and sitting back in the leather chair, "what happened to you? What's happened to Sir Timothy? What was his plan?"

"First of all," began Birrell, setting down his vodka-martini, "let me de-code those Chinese characters you saw on those packing-crates. Mrs. McCracken was very helpful in that."

"There weren't any books in the Frithoway library on Chinese," said Ari, "so I had to go to the British Library yesterday. It was wonderful!"

Birrell took out a crumpled piece of paper and smoothed it out on the desk. "The first one," he explained, "is the Chinese character *Fu*. It means, if you can believe this, *aconite*."

"Aconite is a deadly poison," I pointed out.

"Yes," agreed Birrell, "sweet, but somewhat pungent in flavour."

"Also known as monkshood, wolfsbane, and Queen of Poisons," added Ari.

"And strong flavours will disguise it," said C, "like Sir Timothy's canned foods. Blighter's plan was to poison our chaps on the front line just before a major German offensive."

"What was in the other crates?"

"*Mu fe*," Ari said. "Morphine. Sir Timothy used a distillation of morphine to make the food addictive, so there would be no trouble getting the troops to eat it. That was his plan: get the troops addicted to his food, then lace a shipment with poison right at the moment of a major German offensive."

"Well, I knew he was working for the Germans," I said, "but he said working *with* them, not *for* them. I wonder what he meant by that?"

Fritz, Ari and Birrell exchanged glances, and holding out her glass for a refill on her champagne, Ari said, "I think I can bring a little light to that subject." And she began her story.

CHAPTER 15
ARI'S STORY

When you left that morning (said Ari), the first thing I did was open up the Bible. I didn't care where it opened up, I just opened randomly, like St. Augustine in the garden. I opened it to the letter of St. James: "Go to now, ye rich men, weep and howl in your miseries, which shall come upon you. You have condemned and put to death the Just One; and he resisted you not." I must admit, that scared me at first. I thought you must be the Just One, Mac, and I knew in my heart that Sir Timothy was all bad. But I couldn't get to you, and I needed to protect Archie from him. So I called Fritz, who brought Archie along, and I told him we had to go. He said yes, right away, andmoved toward the dresser. "I shall at once pack the luggage."

"No, we have to go *now*," I repeated.

Fritz's expression didn't change. He just reached into his pocket and checked that there was a round in his pistol. Then he picked up Archie. Archie grumbled a little and rubbed his eyes while I pulled on my boots—you know, the ones I got from that store in New York, the ones that have all the special surprises in the heels.

But just when we were ready to leave, the door opened. In came Charlie McGross, and he had a Luger in his hand. Charlie seemed nervous, and said he'd been instructed to bring all of us to Sir Timothy at once.

"At gunpoint?" I said. "Do you really think that's necessary?"

"I'm sorry, but I think it is." I saw Fritz's hand sliding slowly, almost invisibly towards his pocket. "I don't want to have to use this Luger," said Charlie, "but I will."

"Actually," said Archie, "that's not a Luger. It's a gun."

And there was absolute silence in the room. Charlie's eyes were wide. His face contorted. He looked at Archie, then he looked down at his gun. I could see the conflict raging in him. I prayed and prayed and prayed for him. Then Charlie said in a gasping kind of voice, "You're right, Archie. It's a gun, a filthy gun!" And he threw it across the room.

Then the door opened again, and in came Fr. Jamie. Charlie whirled round and fell to his knees, saying, "Forgive me, Father, for I think I've sinned."

"Well, that's not quite the formula," said Fr. Jamie, pulling out his stole, "and we really should be alone with God, but . . . "

Charlie reached up and seized his hands. "It can wait," he said urgently. "I've been sent to bring you all to Sir Timothy, but I think he has something terrible in mind. He's captured Mr. McCracken."

"He's *what*?" I shouted. "What exactly is he doing to my husband?"

"He's putting him aboard a German submarine," explained Charlie. "I think he wants to take you all to Germany."

"Well, he's not going to do that," I said, pulling out my Derringer. "Which way do we go, Charlie?"

Charlie scrambled to his feet. "This way," he said, pointing through the door. "But shouldn't we get little Archie out of danger?"

"It's where his father is," I replied. "What better place for him?" I had been a bit impatient with Charlie, but now I saw his anguish, and I felt a little guilty. After all, adventuring isn't everyone's family business. "Let's get us all out of danger, shall we, Charlie?" I said, I hope a little more kindly. Then, turning to Fr. Jamie, I asked his blessing. No sooner had Fr. Jamie said "Amen!" than he looked out the window and pointed. "Look!" he said. And there you were—you, Mac, and Sir Timothy and Miss Major and Fr. Kerr and a couple of schoolmasters, all going into the maze.

And then we heard gunfire behind us.

"That's what I came to tell you," said Fr. Jamie. "The castle is under attack—I heard gunfire at the main gate."

So we all dashed out onto the landing. Down below us in the hall we saw a knot of soldiers wearing bonnets, kilts, and very angry expressions. They fanned out, their guns ready for action. Johnnie Birrell was with them

"Mrs. McCracken!" he shouted. "Where is your husband?"

"Sir Timothy is taking him through the maze," I said. I ran down the stairs and joined him in the hall. "There's a U-boat down there in a cave."

Johnnie nodded. "Your husband made a full report, Mrs. McCracken." He pulled out a 1911 Colt. "Let's go."

But we couldn't get out of the building. Two schoolmasters had stationed themselves in the entrance to the maze. They were armed with small machine-guns I'd never seen before—apparently a German model. The Highlanders fired back. I covered Archie's eyes, but Charlie covered him with his own body—God bless him, Charlie's a good man! When I got close, I asked the sergeant in charge, "Have you got Mill's bombs?"

The sergeant frowned. "Yer barms?" He looked at the corporal next to him. "Dougal, d'ye hae this puir Yankee girl's barms?"

The corporal shrugged. "Sergeant," he said, "I dinna ken wha' a barm is."

I took a deep breath and tried to remember Robbie Burns. "Sergeant," I said, "Ah'm askin' ye if ye hae sic a thing as a hand-grenade."

"Och, why did ye no' say so?" He shook his head. "Ah didnae think we'd hae a need fer 'em. Corporal Dougal hefts a wee Lewis gun, ye ken. We hae nothin' bigger."

"Ah ken a Lewis gun is a grand thing," I answered, "but Ah think Ah hae somethin' better!" Now, I knew you'd taken my dynamite, but I still had the glass of tear-gas in the other heel. So I tossed that towards the maze, and there was a bang! and a grey cloud puffed up from where it fell. In a moment, the two schoolmasters staggered out of the maze, coughing and spluttering and clawing at their faces and throats.

So into the maze we charged. At first, I thought we could get through it by looking for the coins you left behind. But of course Sir Timothy had found them. In the end, Corporal Dougal came up, and saluting he said, "Permission tae break rank, sergeant? Ah ken I hae a notion hoo tae get through the booshes."

The sergeant gave him permission and Dougal took off at high speed out of the maze. He returned a couple of minutes later, having liberated a pair of claymores from the walls the hallway in Sir Timothy's castle. "Ah think Ah can clear a wa', sergeant," he said, his eye glinting. He handed one of the claymores to a private and each one crying in a loud voice, "Wallace fer aye!" they hacked and slashed at the bushes, sending up leaves and twigs in such profusion that it looked as if a green cloud hung over them. In no time at all, we found our way to the hut and the chimney. Dougal kicked open the door, and we took the elevator down to the cavern. And that's when we saw everything, Mac, just as you described—all those Chinese crates stacked all over the place and so forth. But I didn't really pay any attention—all I saw was the tail-end of a submarine as it disappeared through a dark archway in the rock all the way across the cavern from us. So I ran towards it, and I fired off both shots from my Derringer, but of course they did no damage to the U-boat.

That was when we heard the voice. "Oh, thank God you're here!" it cried. It was Sir Timothy, who staggered towards us, making the Sign of the Cross. "They just got away—look!" He pointed. By now, the submarine had completely disappeared.

"Where are they taking him?" I snarled, advancing and brandishing my Derringer at him.

Sir Timothy gave a faint sort of giggle. "Mrs. McCracken," he said, "I know you can't do any harm with that—you've had both your shots."

I seized the pistol from Johnnie, and thrust the barrel right between Sir Timothy's eyes. "Where are they taking my husband?" I demanded. My breath came heavily—I was really angry.

Sir Timothy spread his hands. "My dear Mrs. McCracken, I'm so sorry. Your husband and I came down here so I could reassure him I was not up to any kind of nefarious plot, but we found that submarine here, and they took him on board. There was nothing I could do, please believe me!"

I fired a round right over his head. I swear I saw his hair flatten a second as the bullet sped over him. He yelped and jumped backwards, so I fired into the ground just in front of his feet.

"Please, Mrs. McCracken!" he said, putting his hands together in front of him. He had backed right up against a tall stack of crates that wobbled as he touched it. "You must believe me!"

"Why?" I asked. "It's the dumbest lie I've ever heard."

"But I swear it's true. There must be some traitor in my organization."

"Someone close to you, I suppose?" said Fr. Jamie, who had arrived in the second elevator.

"Yes! Someone close to me. Look, I can make all this good. I have plenty of money. I can pay off the Kaiser, and have Mr. McCracken returned in a few weeks."

I looked at Fr. Jamie and Johnnie Birrell. They each wore an expression of utter disgust on their faces. But before any of us could respond to Sir Timothy's outrageous lies, a huge explosion ripped apart the machinery on the far side of the wharf, and we all threw ourselves flat on the concrete floor. Somebody—either Miss Major or Fr. Kerr—had placed some explosives against the deep-fat fryers. It looked like a volcanic explosion, with little balls of fire flying through the air. Sir Timothy was so frightened that he jumped right into the stack of crates, which wobbled again, and then toppled over forward.

* * *

At this point, I gave a gasp. "Right onto Sir Timothy?" I asked.

Ari nodded.

"There weren't that many of them," Fr. Jamie added, "but they did for him all right—I could see that his back was broken." He shook his head sadly. "I got to him as quickly as I could, but I could see at once that he wasnae going to make it. So I said to him, 'Sir Timothy, you've led a bad life, but would you like to make a good end?' Would you believe it? That actually calmed him down. He said he didn't think he could remember everything sinful he'd done, so I told him God would forgive the things he couldn't recall, so long as he was totally honest about everything he could remember. I tell you, Cracky, I've heard many a confession in my life, but that was the one that gave me the greatest joy. Fortunately I had the chrism with me, and he made a good confession before he parted this world."

"And who caused the explosion?" I asked.

"Well, we were able to apprehend Miss Major," explained Birrell, "and she swears she had nothing to do with it."

"Then it was Fr. Kerr?"

"Apparently so," said C. "If so, he perished in the blast—there was no trace of him to be found afterwards."

"And Miss Major told us everything we needed to know about Sir Timothy's plans," said Birrell. "It seems that Sir Timothy really was working for the Bolsheviks. It was quite an elaborate plan. You see, Germany is weak and desperate right now. If they win the War, they will hardly be able to capitalize on their success. Their industry is worn out, their economy in ruins, their people demoralized. Britain will do all right if she wins, but if she loses, then both she and Germany will be spent forces in Europe—ripe for a Communist takeover."

"But Sir Timothy was rich. What could he gain from Communism?"

"Well, Miss Major was fairly clear about that," said C. "What Sir Timothy wanted was an utterly subservient population, and himself in charge. Communism offers the perfect system for such an ambition."

"But I thought communism was all about equality," I protested.

"Yes, everyone thinks that," returned C. "At least, everyone who's been brainwashed to think it. And what better way of brainwashing the people than by infiltrating the schools, by teaching them communism right from the start? Let's face it, you have to really educate people to make them stupid enough to believe all those ridiculous lies."

I gave a low whistle. "He was playing a very long game."

"Well, Mr. McCracken," said C, polishing his monocle, "the long game is really what it's all about, isn't it? We're beginning to realize that the real enemy might not be the Boche at all, but the Bolsheviks. The real war of the next hundred years will be against them, and it won't be fought with battleships and artillery, but with poisoned walking-sticks and code-books."

"Sir?" said Birrell, nudging C. "I believe Mr. Reilly will be waiting for you in Whitehall."

"Hmm. Yes, I expect so." With an expression of distaste, C retrieved his peaked cap from the hook in the hallway while Fritz opened the door for him. "Well, goodbye, Mr. McCracken. I've a feeling we'll be meeting again, and probably quite soon."

And that was the end of that adventure. But another adventure was still continuing.

Chapter 16
An Eleventh-Hour Solution

While we had been in Scotland, much had been happening in Europe. The action I had seen in France was the beginning of what the Germans called the Spring Offensive. For the first time in four years, one side made a significant advance, and it was the Germans, punching a hole through the French and British lines, advancing to less than seventy-five miles from Paris. The shelling I had witnessed in the French capital had been from a massive artillery piece called Big Bertha.

At the same time, the Germans pushed the British north, hoping to expel them from Europe through the northern ports of the English Channel. But the British, who weren't as weak as they had expected, perhaps because they hadn't been poisoned by Sir Timothy's canned food, managed to push them back.

The struggle continued through the summer, with the Allies counter-attacking and driving the Germans slowly and steadily back towards their homeland. Our newspapers were full of reports of how wretched conditions were in Germany—they had no money left, their casualties were mounting, they were running short of arms and ammunition. We all felt that they could not last much longer. And yet they kept on fighting.

Once again, autumn came to England—the fifth autumn of this terrible War. It was, of course, a happy time to us, as our daughter Rosamund had been born in August, and I remember that autumn, the four of us sitting in the parlour of our flat in London. A fire was crackling in the grate, for the day was rather dreary, with low cloud cover and occasional drizzling rain. Archie was perched at the table, like a little olive shoot, seeing how high he could stack his wooden bricks, while Rosamund snoozed peacefully on Ari's shoulder.

"Is there any good news?" asked Ari.

I lowered the newspaper I'd been reading and said, "Just the same old stuff—how bad things are for the Germans. They're surrendering in massive numbers. They're expected to capitulate any day now."

"They've been saying that for weeks."

"Think how bad it would have been if Sir Timothy had succeeded in his plan!" I reminded her.

After a short pause, Ari asked, "Do you ever think of the other one—of Fr. Kerr?"

"Not much," I confessed. "He never seemed very prominent, not till right at the end. He was just in the background, like a shadow."

"And they never found his body," said Ari.

I smiled. "You think he's still alive, planning some other nefarious plot, like Moriarty?"

"I'm sorry that a priest would betray the Church like that. I wonder, whose betrayal came first—Sir Timothy's or Fr. Kerr's?"

"Since they're most likely both dead," I reasoned, "I don't see that it matters much."

Ari was silent for a while. "It shouldn't shake our faith," she said, "that a churchman would betray the people who trusted him. A betrayal like that doesn't change God, and it doesn't affect the truth at all. People betray God all the time, but He doesn't betray them. All the same, they don't know that, and seeing someone like Fr. Kerr sways them, it makes them believe the Church is bad."

"It's true," I admitted, "that disloyalty like that is sort of contagious. But priests are only men. The Church may be divine, but it's staffed by sinful men."

"Of course. But people don't think of that—they just let their prejudice grow."

"They won't ever know about Fr. Kerr," I said. "Like Sir Timothy—the world thinks he died in a yachting accident." Ari didn't look a lot happier. "I know that's not true, but think how damaging it would have been for people to know what he was really planning." I knew that wasn't adequate, I knew in my soul that telling the truth was always the right answer, but I didn't see in this case how that would have worked out. And the official story was already published—devised by someone working for C in Whitehall, and now firmly believed to be the truth by all Sir Timothy's adoring and grieving fans. The victor really did write the history. "I wonder what happened to Sir Timothy's fortune," I added. "C just couldn't get his hands on it, no matter what he tried. All that money just disappeared."

"Money doesn't just disappear," countered Ari. "I would bet anything the Bolsheviks got it."

In the hallway, the clock struck the half-hour. I looked up at a commotion in the street. Rising, I set down the newspaper and crossed to the window.

The street outside was crowded. People rushed to and fro, many of them waving flags. They cheered and ran. Some of them climbed onto a bus that was passing—slowly, for the street was clogged with pedestrians. The top deck of the bus was already jammed with wild, waving passengers.

Fritz joined me at the window. "What's going on, Fritz?" I asked.

Fritz shrugged. "I shall find out, Herr McCracken."

Right outside our flat, a man held up a fizzing bottle of champagne, and poured it into glasses for three or four others. He poured a measure for Fritz, who had just turned up.

Ari, standing beside me with the baby in her arms, said, "Could the War be over?"

"Possibly," I said. "It just seems so . . . " My voice trailed off. "It seems too much to hope for," I concluded lamely.

"Nothing is too much for us to hope for," responded Ari quietly.

The door flew open and Fritz stood there. "Herr McCracken! Frau McCracken! There is peace! There is peace!"

"Peace?"

"*Ja*, peace! It was fifteen minutes ago announced—peace!" Fritz drew a deep breath, quaffed off the rest of his glass of champagne, and said, "Mr. Lloyd George, he announced it fifteen minutes ago—there will be a ceasefire at eleven o'clock. They signed the treaty at five o'clock this morning."

"God be praised!" Ari cried, making the Sign of the Cross.

"They say Mr. Lloyd George will make a public announcement at his house."

"Downing Street? That's just a few blocks away," said Ari.

We bundled into coats and hats, and the three of us, Fritz and myself carrying the children, went out into the street, where the crowd swept us away like a river in spate. I saw a little boy, dressed in red, sounding a bugle—it was the signal for the all-clear after an air-raid, but now it signaled an end to all fighting. All around came the sound of bells—church bells from all over, and above all the notes of Big Ben. "The War is over!" cried a voice, and I saw it belonged to an Australian infantryman, leaning out of a motor-car window, a Union Jack wrapped around his slouch hat. On the bonnet of the car sat a couple of young ladies, waving their arms in the air.

Suddenly, there was a great explosion from the sky, and we all looked up in alarm. It was a natural reaction, after four years of fighting, but in fact it was just a maroon. Another *boom*! and another, but it didn't sound like artillery—it sounded like laughter, pure joy.

One turn, then another, and we were in Downing Street. We stood across the street from Number 10, where the Prime Minister lived. I consulted my watch. It was ten minutes to eleven.

"We want Lloyd George!" cried a voice, and it was soon joined by another and another, until it became a chant.

Then the door to the balcony opened, and the Prime Minister stepped out. The crowd roared, like a stormy sea. Mr. Lloyd George held up a hand. He was a small, almost disheveled man in his late fifties with a bushy moustache. He smiled as the noise of the crowd died down.

"I am glad to tell you," he said in his Welsh accent, "that the War will be over at eleven o'clock today!"

A roar of jubilation went up from the crowd. More fireworks exploded overhead. Two boys blew bugles from just in front of us. Archie was excited. Someone had given him a little flag, and he waved it vigorously. Rosamund was upset, though, and Ari had taken her from Fritz to comfort her.

"Remember this moment, Archie," I said. "This is a very great moment."

The last of the fireworks faded, and Mr. Lloyd George had been joined by his wife Margaret, Mr. Winston Churchill, and Mr. Bonar Law, the Chancellor of the Exchequer.

"You are well entitled to rejoice," said the Prime Minister, raising his voice above the crowd. He waited a moment, his eyes sparkling. When the noise had subsided a little, he added, "The people of this Empire, with their Allies, and the people of the Dominions of India, have won a great victory for humanity. It is the sons and daughters of the people who have done it. They have won this hour of gladness, and the whole country has done its duty. It has achieved a triumphant victory, which the world has never seen before." And raising his voice, he concluded: "Let us thank God!" The housemaids of Downing Street, leaning out of their windows, waved mops and feather dusters, while jubilant Government clerks, men and women, clambered onto the ridged rooftops of the Foreign Office.

And a joyous roar broke out, while Ari, Fritz and I all crossed ourselves. Ari, I could see, was weeping silently. Stooping down a little, I kissed my wife and said, "Come on, I'll buy you some champagne."

THE END

From Fritz's Kitchen

Cullen Skink

Ingredients

1 ¼ pints milk
1 tsp. parsley
1 bay leaf
1 pound smoked haddock
2 tbs. butter
1 onion, finely chopped
8 oz. mashed potatoes
Salt and pepper (to taste)

Directions

1. Place milk, parsley, bay leaf, and haddock into a large saucepan, reserving ½ tsp. parsley for later.
2. Bring milk to a gentle boil and simmer for 3 mins.
3. Remove the pan from the heat and leave for 5 mins. The herbs will their flavour infuse into the milk.
4. Remove haddock from milk with a slotted spoon and put to one side.
5. Strain liquid through a fine sieve and reserve herb-infused milk.

6. Heat the butter in another, smaller saucepan. Add the onions and cook gently until translucent, about 5 mins. Do not burn them!
7. Add milk and potato to onions and stir until incorporated and a thick, creamy consistency.
8. Break up haddock into small chunks; make sure you remove any bones you find. Add to the soup.
9. Add reserved parsley to soup and simmer gently 4-5 mins. Do not stir too much, or you will break up haddock much.
10. Add salt and pepper as needed.
11. Garnish soup with reserved parsley or perhaps a little extra pepper.

Bannock

Ingredients

3 cups flour
1 tsp. salt
2 tbsp. baking powder
¼ cup butter, melted
1½ cups water

Directions

1. Measure flour, salt, and baking powder into a large bowl. Stir to mix. Pour melted butter and water over flour mixture. Stir with fork to make a ball.

2. Turn dough out on a lightly floured surface, and knead gently about 10 times. Pat into a flat circle ¾ to 1 inch thick.
3. Cook in a greased frying pan over medium heat, allowing about 15 mins. for each side. Or you may bake the bannocks on a greased baking sheet at 350 degrees F for 25 to 30 minutes.

About the Author

Like the famous Cat, Mark Adderley was born in Che-shire, England. His early influences included C. S. Lewis and adventure books of various kinds, and his teacher once wrote on his report card, "He should go in for being an author," advice that stuck with him. He studied for some years at the University of Wales, where he became interested in medieval literature, particularly the legend of King Arthur. But it was in graduate school that he met a clever and beautiful American woman, whom he moved to the United States to marry. He spent some time as a professor of literature, and is now the Director of Religious Education at the St. Thomas More Newman Center at the University of South Dakota. He is the author of a number of novels about King Arthur for adults, and originally wrote the McCracken books for his younger two children.

Made in the USA
Middletown, DE
23 December 2021